I0682948

"280"

Jeremy Rafuse

First published in 2024 by Blossom Spring Publishing
"280" Copyright © 2024 Jeremy Rafuse
ISBN 978-1-0685693-8-8
E: admin@blossomspringpublishing.com
W: www.blossomspringpublishing.com
All rights reserved under International Copyright Law.
Contents and/or cover may not be reproduced in whole
or in part without the express written consent of the publisher.
Names, characters, places and incidents are either products
of the author's imagination or are used fictitiously.

For my mom

Table of Contents

Boulder

There is blood on the table, the floor, and a significant amount on the walls.

Marco goes over to the corner of the room and finds one counterman still mumbling as he lies with his face scrunched against the wall. He crouches down beside him, twists his head, and shoots him once more in the mouth.

There is an unmistakable sense of power that they share. And then, suddenly, they are new people, and they have little time for each other. Indeed, Marco notices, he raises his hand to his ear, trying to listen to the sounds outside the conference room. Or else Hana holds her hand on her chest, and walks in an awkward gait, almost as though trying to say she was not capable of this kind of human destruction.

They are mesmerized by the speed of their kill. This is the mess that semi-automatic guns make, with silencers. A high-powered shampoo vacuum system is in use in the hallway, just like Marco planned.

Detaching from spraying death on people is proving difficult. But Hana insists they revel in their cruelty, and she appears to treat the dead as test ground to improve their reputation as famous criminals.

She places the duffle bags full of money on the pushcart. They go over to the door and pause before deciding what to do next.

Marco checks his watch, and he knows they are under the gun. It is only a matter of time before the police arrive. So far, however, no slips.

He turns towards Hana and takes her in his arms. He is still shaking from all the shooting. He holds her tight, and as he looks over her shoulder – at the conference table, the dead bodies – it feels like a dream.

The bodies show a side of death few people see, namely the dead who are committed to a life of crime, and so they are always living a dress rehearsal anyway. The expressions are comic, as though the more serious dead are only found in the movies.

They make their way to the parking lot. A van rolls up and two men jump out, load the van, and quickly drive off.

The police arrive. Marco wants to stand out. He gets in their faces. He searches for Hana.

They sit inside a minivan and answer questions for what seems like forever. But they have mastered their story. They listen to the police and follow orders. They are plotting their next job.

After an intense interrogation, Marco steps outside for a cigarette, where he notices one of the detectives.

The detective wears a navy suit and burgundy Oxfords. His hands and neck are thick, and he has the strangest disposition. That is, even though he can admit he is an expert on Boulder, there is an unnerving detachment which makes him look even tougher and stronger, as though he is an expert on numerous neighborhoods all over the States. But it is bittersweet; he once called Boulder his home turf, but now it is just another anonymous crime scene.

Marco had set it up so fifty or so witnesses saw him in the pool during the murders. The entire operation must have cost the Italian mob a small fortune.

Finally, Marco and Hana are allowed to go home. There is a veil of suspicion about their presence. But that is only for the outsiders. As far as the investigation is concerned, they have been cleared as suspects. They have an innocuous presence, and soon look like tourists. Some people even feel sorry for Marco – that he would have to live through something so traumatic, where eleven people were killed.

The next day, they take a long drive. Marco orders two cheeseburgers, fries, and Cokes. He goes over to the gas station and buys a newspaper.

Eleven dead, execution style.

Hana has a big smile on her face, and it is not because they have evaded the cops, but because her cheeseburger is so good. The fries have been cooked in dirty oil. The Coke is on the sugary side, with crushed ice. Hana removes a daddy long legs from Marco's chest, and hands him his burger. Hana watches the cars coming and going in the background. The slam of the restaurant's serving window is a reminder that they are at a famous destination.

They sit in the rental car and listen to the radio. The local station covers the murder at the hotel. They have tapped into a part of the American psyche that is always present, but is never to be found, except now. And there is a humorous side to what happened. As the news is reported – the description of the location, how many police and ambulances are on the scene, the number of dead – the personalities reporting the tragedy all begin to assume an unreal quality. It will not be long before kids are starting to poke fun at the hotel murders. Soon there will be knee slaps at the local tavern. The story will be repeated over and over in the workplace, at the universities, and soon it will become part of the American psyche.

Marco takes a sip of his Coke and looks at Hana.

"We cannot utter a word about this to anyone."

"I know."

"As long as you're happy, I'm happy. I love you and that's all that matters."

Japan

The captain announces they will be landing shortly in Tokyo. The Air Japan stewardess taps Marco on the shoulder and awakens him. He has come all the way from Rome, his hometown, to meet Hana, his girlfriend of six months. Marco ponders if it is possible to fall in love with someone at a tech conference; Hana seems to think they are just going through the motions, but she wants to see where it goes.

At the afterparty, they wear floral, plastic necklaces, and name tags in thick, black marker, like on The *Price is Right*. Hana takes the celery garnish from Marco's Bloody Caesar and inconspicuously skips it across the dance floor.

The plane is full of mostly tourists returning home from a once-in-a-lifetime vacation in Italy. Marco appraises the solemn, pious faces as he gently lifts his brown, Gucci bag from the overhead compartment. And the passengers are caught staring adoringly at Marco, as though he represents a walk-on from an Antonioni film.

There are some challenges to being in a mixed relationship. In Boulder, however, they liked the differences. It offered the young couple a layer of mystery. At first, they spoke in broken English, but soon they were using hand gestures and had even started to build an impressive repertoire of slang, which only they understood, begetting an even stronger bond.

Ultimately, neither one cares very much about their linguistic side. The cumbersome moments are worth it.

And they have mastered the skills to eavesdrop, interject, say something which, at times, is more powerful than language.

Clearly marked signs hang from the ceiling, a row of metal benches line the airport passageway, a robotic cleaner pushes the emotional energy forward.

Once you leave a job you have no further responsibilities. Let's say you're called upon to pull a bank heist, and you take out one of the tellers (he or she gets in the way), once you're in the getaway car, it's all long forgotten.

They stopped using FaceTime several months back, as it was causing Hana too many sleepless nights.

The clank of the baggage carousel, the boom of a sliding glass door, and the perturbed murmur of airport visitors in an awkward dance with departures or arrivals.

Hana falls to her knees and begins to cry. Her hands tremble. Marco reaches for her and falls on his knees and kisses her on the forehead.

The stop signs are triangular. The overpass signs are yellow with green letters. Look at the neatness of the Tokyo storefronts. And Hana smiles with amusement at all of Marco's observations. Marco notes how serious and professional everyone looks. Hana assumes an air of importance. She is protective and inquisitive. They clutch hands, and dance with their bodies against each other. The taxi driver curses. Or a cyclist leans his knobby arm against the side of the taxi. They are heading for Hana's parents' home.

Some of the biggest troublemakers in the past have

been neighbors. We have seen cases where someone was set up in a domestic situation, only to meet a nosey neighbor. If that happens, make a quick getaway and start all over again.

A friendly face, alert ears, and gentle disposition. Sota, who is a Shiba Inu, is red sesame, and acts uncontrollably around Marco, jumping and barking, and making a real mess in every direction. Sota especially likes to nibble at the bottom of Marco's rayon trousers. Marco speaks Italian to Sota, but the generous Italian phrasing tends to aggravate matters, and Hirato, Hana's father, ends up trying to get the dog's attention.

The cultural differences tend to calm the awkwardness. Midori, Hana's mother, does not have any regrets about the conservative introductions. Or else Hirato covers some of the missteps. Even Sota, the punctilious house dog, appears to sidestep the loopy introductions.

Midori is wrinkly, despite only being in her early fifties. She lives in a world of distraction; she shuffles her sweater arms, or else darts a glance towards the other room. Hirato smiles politely at his wife, who untangles her necklace and begins to speak frantically to Hana, completely ignoring Marco.

Out of nervousness, Marco continues to speak to Sota in Italian.

It does not work well around the house, creating jitters among the group. Hirato enters the dining room and sits down on the wooden chair with a red satin back. He transfers his glass of white wine from hand to hand, focussing on Sota.

Hirato falls to his knees, and crawls towards Sota and

7

speaks a few gentle words in Japanese. Next, he begins to raise his voice, which causes little barks.

Hirato was in his twenties at the time, and his wife was recently pregnant.

One day, a Yakuza boss came over to his house and knocked at the door. Hirato was told he now owns a restaurant in Utsunomiya, in Northern Japan. He had to start work immediately.

"What does that mean?"

"It means we own a restaurant, and we need you to take care of the day-to-day operations."

Hirato explained the situation to Midori. They quickly packed the car and moved the two hundred miles to Utsunomiya.

The restaurant had been closed for a few weeks. It specialised in dumplings, specifically the yaki-gyoza style, and yakisoba (stir fry noodles). The shop was also famous for the Kikkoman Soy Sauce, which was made with a secret chili oil recipe. Hirato got the names of all the former staff, and quickly hired them back. Within no time they were all back in business. Through connections, Hirato was able to get a liquor licence, and at night he turned the restaurant into a bar.

Within a very short amount of time, he was making money hand over fist.

But all during this time, no one told him why he was running a restaurant. He was simply asked to do his duty and keep busy working. And then one day, someone entered the restaurant.

The man, who said his name was Goro, explained he was from a local gang: the Suzumebachi. He demanded that Hirato pay him a monthly protection tax going forward. Hirato promptly took Goro to the back of the restaurant and killed him. He disposed of the body. A few days later, another man came by the restaurant and told Hirato that he must pay the protection tax, or his life would be at risk. Hirato took the man to the back of the restaurant and killed him.

The Suzumebachi had now lost two of their more important enforcers and demanded compensation. But Hirato refused to budge. In fact, he denied the whole story.

Then, one day, while Hirato was out buying food for the restaurant, he was stopped by the leader of the Suzumebachi, Isamu, who said he wanted to talk to clear the air. The two men decided to go for bubble tea at a local restaurant, where they could shoot the breeze. Hirato was asked point blank "where are the two bodies?" Hirato repeated over and over that he was not responsible for the two missing gangsters.

"Where did they go?"

Hirato scratched the side of his face, and then looked deep into the eyes of the man opposite him.

"I don't know. Maybe you have a problem with gang members deserting their life and starting out fresh?"

"These were degenerate killers. They settle scores for drug deals gone bad. They are not interested in opening a cabana in Florida."

"Well, it's very hard for me to understand why you would come to me and think that I am a killer, when you know damn well, I'm a simple restaurant owner."

The two men returned to Hirato's restaurant.

Isamu smoked a joint and wandered around the restaurant and there was an unmistakable feeling of revenge. At any moment, Isamu could have removed a gun and killed Hirato. But Hirato held to his story and denied the whole thing. Next, Isamu went over to the bar and took a stool, whereupon Hirato instinctively went to the kitchen side and started making Isamu dumplings. Isamu drank four Sapporo beers, and then got quite drunk on whiskey. By the time Isamu was about to leave, the slate had been cleaned. Hirato, of course, did not charge Isamu for his meal and drinks, and sent him off with the feeling that he was rather impressed he had come over to discuss business. Isamu stopped in the doorway. He turned and looked at Hirato.

"Perhaps you didn't kill them. They were bastards anyways. But at least I know where I can have a drink and rest my soul every once in a while."

Hirato closed the restaurant. Midori greeted him at the front door. There was a silent agreement that Hirato had escaped death. But given all the death that had happened lately, there was also a sense of disgust about their union. The drama created a new atmosphere, a new sensibility between the couple.

Midori thought Hirato was a target; that the meeting with Isamu was just a decoy, a way to build anger for the Suzumebachi. Soon they would pounce. Hirato emphasized how sincere Isamu had acted, but Midori would not have any of it. Indeed, she spent a moment explaining that she knew Hirato better than he knew himself, and that she refused to sit around and worry about whether or not he was going to get himself killed, because it was bound to happen. She insisted that Hirato was not taking life seriously enough. In other words, they had to leave at once.

The Yakuza hoped that Hirato would come to his senses and build the restaurant, but Hirato told them he was not able to be that type of gangster. He was more useful as someone who stands in a doorway on a dark street and snatches a purse. The Yakuza would see his departure as an insult, but in the face of death, which he hid from his bosses, he had no other choice but to leave.

He explained that his family needed him back in Tokyo. He had been hired to work at Suzuki.

"But you are part of our family!"

There was a great silence, but it turned uncomfortable because Hirato had successfully built up the restaurant, and even created a profitable bar. But more importantly, he had put fear in the hearts of the Suzumebachi.

They would have preferred to kill him than let him go, but they lacked the means to explain their true feelings. And, besides, the profits from the restaurant would erase any association going forward. Indeed, his boss looked around the room at his partners, and then decided to speak some embarrassing words.

"You have become a legend in our circles. We wish you success in your new adventures. And always remember that you have a home to come back to."

Midori cried for weeks, believing they had performed a miracle. She made Hirato his lunch for his shift at Suzuki. Hopefully, the family would grow and prosper and distance themselves more and more from the Yakuza as time went by.

Marco and Hana have created many layers in their relationship. They wince at the cultural hang-ups some people might have. And soon they are bemused by what outsiders might think of their relationship. Even down to their skin complexions, the flow of their hair, eye colors.

Marco considers his black hair and dark complexion

rather ordinary. Hana has not always liked her look. She once considered Asian blepharoplasty surgery so she could look more like Winona Ryder from *Stranger Things*. Midori bungled that idea, and today it remains a somewhat humorous anecdote in the family, where Hana was once nearly disowned.

Hirato mentions World War II. Hana is already bored by the mention of war.

Midori places some chicken *katsu* on his plate, which is crispy chicken rolled in panko breadcrumbs. Hirato hands Marco a little dish of tangy, brown sauce.

Neither one studied history during university. Their superficial knowledge about the war provides them just enough information to keep their ideas in check. They are aware they were not on the winning side of the war.

But the events surrounding Pearl Harbour are much bigger than simple dinner conversation. Hirato recommends the young couple visit Hiroshima.

Hana is finally accepted for a job after she fills out an online questionnaire. The hiring committee is impressed that Hana had some banking experience. They immediately hire her for the Boulder job. She once worked a job in Eugene, Oregon, where she was in charge of a jewel heist. She ended up killing the owner of the jewellery shop. Consequently, her trust metrics are not as high as they should be. But her banking experience helped her in the present case, and she is likely to be rehired for future roles if she continues to work jobs as they are arranged at the outset.

The thought of revisiting Hiroshima remains a private affair. Hana has no intention of inviting her parents. She sees the day trip as an opportunity to get closer to Marco.

"If you don't like house rules, you can find a motel."

They decide to watch a Rolling Stones documentary on Netflix, but soon after they are too busy making out to pay attention. Suddenly, Marco looks up and sees Hirato in the doorway, dancing in his underpants to *Jumping Jack Flash*.

His back is covered in a dragon. And it appears to swoop around to his front and ends up on the left shoulder. It almost looks like the snake is resting. Or, from another angle, the dragon is about to rip the head off its host.

And then there are the flowers, the cherry blossoms, which are displayed on all the parts of his body, behind his knees and elbows, and they act like a bed for the dragon to slither about. And then there is the mighty tiger, who represents strength, however his presence is almost invisible.

And slithering through the gaps are a variety of snakes, which represent healing. Overall, they make the tattoo appear self-sufficient and capable of defending itself. The entire piece is vibrantly inked in white and black, an inviting blue, and touches of red, yellow, and green.

Hana jumps up, grabs the old-fashioned glass full of whiskey, and helps her father into bed.

The young couple attend a music festival. Hana wants to show Marco a side of Tokyo that outsiders normally never see. The music scene is indescribable, from rock to jazz and everything in-between. There are food trucks, and numerous stages playing music from all around the world. The entrance area feels like the cross-roads of the universe.

Tsumugi had appeared during Hana's teenage years. They used to skip class and spend the afternoons at the arcade. They read the Beat Generation together, and that pretty much turned them into fast friends. Now, the two school mates perform a little introductory dance, and then give each other a longish hug. Hana introduces Tsumugi to Marco. His hand appears caught in his hair, unsure how to comport himself during introductions. And yes, he acknowledges, the Japanese are polite, but he feels awkward to the point of hilarity: overwhelmed by nervousness. Hana makes the introductions for both of her friends.

Tsumugi concedes she is a natural when it comes to speaking English, when she has no natural talents in anything else. She had travelled to Toronto, Canada, and studies at the University of Toronto, at the Scarborough campus, taking a full load of philosophy courses. She connects with other Japanese students at the International Students Association. She had won second prize at the Toastmaster Club for a talk on pollution in space.

All of the hard work learning English had not helped her in her career. Indeed, her job at Google requires no English whatsoever. She spends a few nights a week watching YouTube vids, but the punchy Brit comedy skits like *Mr. Bean* and *The Vicar of Dibley* are starting to bore her. Her attention is focussed more and more on Japanese things these days.

Some of the best players are those who have formed friendships in their domestic lives. If any of their friends

14

become suspicious, you must deal with the situation accordingly. As your social network grows, the easier a player can rest.

The music blasts, the aromas of an open BBQ, Hana and Tsumugi finally remove the bandana covering Marco's eyes. Marco falls to the ground and rolls with laughter. Hana wears fluorescent sunglasses. Hana and Tsumugi hold a can of Bud which they puncture, and shotgun in unison, the drink dispensing in a few seconds. They finish with a series of selfies.

In Boulder, she blocks him from returning to the hotel. She looks at the fleet of cars in the parking lot. A group of tourists disembarks from an airport shuttle. A parking lot attendant lights a cigarette. Next, Hana kisses Marco. They remain inside their luxury room for two days. And postpone the job twice.

Back at Hana's parents' house, she sits up and tries to watch an episode of *Downton Abbey*. Midori tells Hana how much she likes Marco. After all, he is a young John Travolta. Hana laughs, because she only knows Travolta from *Pulp Fiction,* shooting up heroin. Marco asks Hana to come back to Rome…to begin something.

They exit the three-star Boulder hotel. They begin to bicker. And their voices start to get louder and louder. And now they are shouting. Hana admits her dad is Yakuza, and she likes to name drop, like some spiffy BBC intellectual. Marco puts his hands on his knees, and he has trouble breathing. The hotel is in the background. Hana breaks into a safe place, and says she will call her contact, and the plan can go forward.

We are considered an important crime syndicate. But we keep a low profile. There are some people who doubt that we even exist. That's the way we like it.

We put word on the street that we needed to raise some money. For each party interested, it is a two-million-dollar investment, with a substantial return within one year and impressive royalties for a maximum of ten years.

We didn't care who was attached, or how many people for that matter. All we wanted was to collect the two million dollar asking price.

Six investors came forward. All of the different parties believed they were the primary investor. Either they would work as a team, or else, quite possibly, they would decide to cut each other's throats.

The six groups include: Marco from Rome, Italy, Hana from Tokyo, Japan, two brothers from Delaware, a trio from Australia, a trio from Russia, and a hotel owner from Mumbai, India.

Delaware and Australia put a lot of money on the street to find out who was attending.

We discovered that India and Russia were content to show some muscle. The Russians claimed they were in the hole after a botched car smuggling scheme. Apparently, they lost millions after the police set up a sting operation in the Northeastern United States and along the St. Lawrence in Canada.

The Indian crew simply wanted to boost their image.

Our biggest worry was Delaware and Australia. Both crews had spent a fortune to try and sniff out how the plan would go down. Good word had it that they were going to join forces and split the upfront costs. But we also heard they were interested in making a deal. One crew in New York City set up a meeting. Both crews paid one hundred thousand dollars for the meeting. The New York crew offered up five paintings – early French impressionism, which could easily fetch over one hundred million at auction – to be part of the deal. The problem, however, would be getting the paintings on the auction table. Gangsters like art because they can exchange famous paintings against a lengthy prison sentence. Prosecutors tend to make these deals, because they can tell the press they foiled an art fraud ring.

Delaware and Australia both ended up walking away from the deal because it was too dangerous. They decided to split the costs between themselves and roll with the punches.

The Australia crew decide to scout things out and find out how they should play their cards.

The Delaware crew go out to Burger King, and then over to a strip bar. The Australia crew trail them to the bar, and just when they are about to pounce, they are caught in the act.

The Australians stumble upon the Italian man and Japanese lady. They are attending a technology conference. Again, the Australians are pinched by the Italian, who has a huge crew with him. Everyone believed the Italian was working alone, but he has a crew bigger than the University of Colorado's offensive line. The Australians insist they partner up, and it looks like Marco is going to make the deal, but just as they are about to shake on it, he takes a call, and then suddenly the deal is off the table.

The Australians return to the hotel where the Russian and Indian crews are waiting for them in the bar. Daphne, the hotel clerk, is in tatters. One of the Australians tips her one hundred dollars. She runs back to the front desk.

The Russians remove their guns.

The Russian mobster has a long, hooked nose, and straight hair, with a cowlick at the front, which creates a strange parting in his hair.

He is not athletic, but his rake thinness makes him appear as though he could have been a decent athlete if he had put in the effort. His forearms are covered in Russian mob prison tattoos. One arm has a portraiture of Stalin, surrounded by images of farmers, which look like Van Gogh characters.

He is from central or eastern Russia – the Siberian part of the mighty country. He is at ease in his own skin, but really doesn't have much taste for living, and prefers to use drugs, visit prostitutes, and fight whenever he gets the chance. By chance he becomes an important mobster and makes good money. However, it is purely accidental, and the illegal riches of being a mobster reflect poorly on his character.

Next, the business owners from Mumbi, who wear sharp suits and have distinctive moustaches, remove their guns. Suddenly, there is a funny situation, because the Russians didn't expect the heat. The Australian pulls out a grenade, and then things start to get interesting. The problem is that no one understands what the others are saying. Finally, the Australian says they have some property in Australia, and they should all partner up. The Russians immediately cool down. The Indians, however, have a different idea. They are ready to kill. But there is no escape. The front desk clerk, Daphne, enters the bar, sees everyone, and almost faints. She races back to the lobby and calls the police.

Suddenly, it is gunfight at the OK Corral.

One hour later, Daphne is found dead in the back of the hotel, in the garbage container. The bartender acts frozen when he is interviewed by the police. He tells the police he didn't see anything during his shift, save he made a lot of rum and Cokes. Strangely, all of the CCTV footage goes missing.

The next morning, all of the gangsters read in the *Boulder Citizen* about the dead hotel clerk. They act upset, as though something like that could never happen at their lodgings.

Meanwhile, Marco sits in his Boulder hotel room and contemplates different scenarios. He makes a phone call and tells his contact he is intending to make a hit. Someone relays back that it is ok. Ultimately it is a Sicilian connection that has to approve the hit. Marco's family has never had ties with the Sicilian mafia, but they are the ones who are in charge in this kind of situation. In other words, if Marco is successful, there needs to be a plan to protect Marco upon his return. His family do not have the resources to provide this cover. This is why the Sicilians are so efficient. They offer protection for a small fee. It is the Sicilian way of saying "thank you for being a cold-blooded killer, but we're charging you a tax fee for the service".

Hana has been busy making arrangements.

Hana decides to forgo her plans to make a name for herself. She has fallen in love with Marco. She takes a call from back home which asks her to take care of business and confirms that she is not allowed to partner up with anyone. She tries to explain the connection she has with Marco, yet no one seems interested. She insists that Marco is a good contact. His family is well connected – he is a gateway into the European market. There is a long silence, and then someone else comes on the line and tells Hana she is ordered to take out Marco and the others. A representative in the parking lot will help her collect the money.

Hana hangs up the phone and it dawns on her there is no reasonable way out of her situation. She makes a phone call for the car to be brought around the front. They drive the short distance to the hotel. She grabs the duffle bag from the trunk, puts it on the trolley, and then walks casually towards the front entrance.

Marco has not mentioned marriage, but he has hinted that he is interested in planning a life together. She does not understand what Marco wants. She is hosting him while he is in Japan. And they are indefinite about marriage. Hana is not willing to host his fancy in Japan, or else, even more exceptional, go to Rome, simply to see how things develop.

Hana is getting antsy. She does not want to host Marco in Japan anymore while he decides what they are going to do next. Or else "build" on their relationship and venture to Rome and see how things develop. Hana decides to establish some rules, create an ultimatum in their relationship or, at the very least, ask that Marco be more specific about what he wants to do next.

Marco decides to go outside and sit on the little picnic table. He is about to light a Seven Star when the door opens. The *Ichiju Sansai* format includes a piece of fish,

Shiru, which is a soup, *Kounomono* pickles, *gohan*, and two side dishes, veg and an egg dish. It looks more impressive than his graduation dinner at the University of Roma.

The door closes behind her, whereupon she places two fresh croissants into a small basket, returns to the terrace, and offers them to Marco.

He is flattered by the attention of his new family, and he agrees that things are going according to plan. But there remain some awkward moments, like walking through the house, and not knowing what to say if he encounters someone. Or the impossibility of breaking the monotony with a single comment. Marco feels unprotected. But that is part of the process – one of the pitfalls of falling in love. He climbs the stairs, the thick carpet between his toes, and the bookcase on the landing holding Japanese literature, like Murasaki Shikibu, Yukio Mishima, and the works of Haruki Murakami.

Midori comes from a family very much confused about the war. Her grandfather on her father's side, Haru Watanabe, was in World War II and will spend the rest of his life recounting the horrors, knowing that the Japanese were on the wrong side of history. He says he must make up for all the wrongs his government did during the war. He highlights the atrocities in Europe. He says he completely understands why the Americans dropped the bomb. They were under tremendous pressure, and Japan was not about to give up.

Haru's son, Minato, takes on a much different attitude. He listened to his father with undivided attention and learned a great deal about the world through his eyes. But, in the end, he took a different approach towards the war. He thinks his father was indoctrinated to think that the Japanese were in the wrong.

Once Midori got older, she was unsure what to believe. On the one hand, she respected her grandfather's position. But, on the other hand, she respected her father's interpretation, which was a less popular view to take.

In the end, it remains inner toil for Midori to decide where to stand about the war. Even though the war has ended, she feels like she is the inheritor of a problem, and she must come up with her own answers.

Haru was a uniformed soldier in Hirohito's air force, which stood shoulder to shoulder with Hitler's Germans, and supported the myth to conquer the world.

She understands that her father had to listen to his father's war stories incessantly. He was expected to assume his father's sensibilities. But that was an impossible task: the war machine was far more complex than that.

Her grandfather was a fighter pilot, who piloted the Kawasaki Ki-45. He flew hundreds of missions, and likely shot down numerous enemy aircraft (Midori does not know this for certain as Haru never admitted he killed anyone). There was a kind of fairness in the way he participated in the war. In other words, he was ordered to fly aircraft and fight the Americans, Canadians, and British. He took his role seriously. Also, he was not aware of the atrocities committed by his government or the axis powers. Haru admits he felt proud fighting for his country, but in hindsight he questions the authenticity of his own feelings.

Time changes public opinion. Or else, there is the tendency to take on a controversial view about the war.

Most people would keep their ideas private, but there is always a transformative understanding about war, because it is so utterly wrong to begin with.

Minato supports Japan's position during the war. He believes that his father is a war hero, who successfully shot down many American, British, and Canadian fighters.

Haru cannot understand why his son would oppose his true feelings. Minato, on the other hand, cannot understand why his father would deny him the belief that his father is a hero.

One day, Haru told his son that they should not discuss the war anymore.

"If a man rapes a woman, and then he is arrested, and shown what he has done, don't you think it is reasonable that he should admit he was wrong? Why are you so obtuse!"

Minato turned on his father and chose to pursue the opposite lifestyle: namely a life of crime. It is important to note that Minato never properly explained to anyone why he decided to turn against his father. Midori blames World War II putting such a strain on her family that it made it impossible for the family to communicate.

"There is nothing else to speak about after the concentration camps."

"Yes, there is my life, your life, the Japanese people's lives."

"There is no life after the concentration camps. The concentration camps ended life as we know it. A system of death was used, and our best minds created it. There is no turning back. We have failed ourselves."

"But you can speak, you are speaking. You must find a way to continue to speak."

Minato explains that the war is a great masquerade of lies. No one told the truth. And yet the truth is always known. Once the war ends, news starts to spread about the concentration camps. And it comes as no surprise to most people. Indeed, the world acknowledge the killing in their daily walks.

Minato becomes a high-level enforcer in several gangs in Japan. He kills people for not paying their debts. He spends time in prison but is eventually released because his lawyers are smart and know all the right things to say.

In the upstairs hallway, Marco examines the bookcase. He feels unprotected. He feels distant from his home. But, he admits, these are the pitfalls of falling in love.

Marco goes over to Hana who lies on the couch.

"If you don't get up now, you might never want to get up."

"I know."

Hana falls to the ground and grabs one of Marco's ankles. She pulls herself towards him and kisses the side of his shin. Marco reaches down, cups Hana's head in his hands, and then kisses her on the neck. She begins to laugh and shakes her head like he is in the front row of a Beatles concert.

"I think we should go to Hiroshima."

"Why?"

"Because I think I'm falling in love with you, and we need something like a Hiroshima as a backdrop to remember this experience."

They board the *Shinkansen*, a bullet train that runs from Okayama to Hiroshima in forty minutes.

The stiff train seats and hard glass. Cool air stretches

up the window to give the appearance of perfection: they are model riders.

The fact that his face turns red does not at all mean that he is jealous. Indeed, he recognizes he needs to brush up on his Japanese. He does, however, recognize that this is the type of Westerner the Japanese people prefer to see. He is the one that comes from Pennsylvania, Paris, or London, who speed reads the *Sekai Nippo* or *The Japan Times*, and offers endless commentary afterwards.

And his relationship with Hana grows stronger. But he needs more opportunities to speak Japanese, and to immerse himself more into the culture, like the big wigs around him who will someday turn into strangers.

They arrive at the Hiroshima Peace Memorial, the Genbaku Dome. Designed in 1915 by the Czech architect Jan Letzel, it symbolises strength and occupies a special place in Hiroshima.

The site of destruction is surrounded by modern buildings. Its emptiness, indirect lighting, and dome structure, void of a roof, extol the vulnerable side of human ingenuity: how beautiful things can be destroyed. And it looks more Japanese than all the other buildings.

Hana looks at Marco, the skeletal remains of a building, and the bright sky flash shadows every which way.

It is a quick reference from her father at the dinner table. Hirato does not want to disrupt Hana's expensive education. Nor does he think he can outthink her private schoolteachers. And besides, Hana will find out sooner or later and eventually resent her father for putting undue pressure on her to think a particular way. She needs some other way to understand this place. Hana stares at the building and waits... and waits. Finally, she begins to cry. Marco does not have a proper response, but he somehow understands her grieving. He holds her in his arms, with a slight breeze, even the noise of distant traffic, eases their mood.

Marco thinks about Italy and its role just before Hiroshima was bombed in 1945. His mom, Serena, was born in 1960. She has pictures of her father, and he wears a uniform with the fascist government images.

The Germans share a bed with all the "neutral" countries, which include Sweden, Spain, Italy, Portugal, and everywhere in-between. The Swedes provide iron for the Nazi war machine. The Portuguese feed the Nazi soldiers sardines.

Serena developed mixed feelings for her Italian background. And today she remains mistrustful of politics. Instead, she embraces Christianity. Her Catholic faith is not motivated by love, but rather as a destination, away from fascist thinking. Whenever she goes to church, it is not to pray to God, but rather to shut the door on fascist ideology.

In a rather dark and oblique way, Hana and Marco are in competition with one another to show off their lives. And in Hiroshima, Hana has the upper hand. The visceral reactions are mushy, but the feelings quickly transform, from a never-ending cloud to the other places that resemble this kind of evil. She knows about the tens of thousands of work, labour, and concentration camps in Europe, but no nuclear weapons are used in those places.

As she looks at him, or touches his hair, and he wraps his arm around her slender shoulders, suddenly the ideas of war change. Marco is suitable to touch because they are in a similar situation. She feels scared, apprehensive that perhaps they are nurturing a part of themselves that should remain silent.

And none of her friends, as far as she can recall, would ever speak out against Japan's role in the war. Her family defends Japan's reputation. It is important to always remember the Japanese war dead.

The government of Japan only found out about the blast after listening to reports from Washington. On August 06 1945, at 08:15 a.m., in the city of Hiroshima in the southern part of Japan, a well-known military base was destroyed. Prior to the attack, the population of Hiroshima was two hundred and fifty-five thousand. Hiroshima suffered sixty-six thousand deaths and sixty-nine thousand injuries: a total of one hundred and thirty-five thousand casualties.

Across the main square, Marco and Hana find an irregular-shaped bench, with a high, slatted back. They sit down with their Subway Subs, cookies, and fountain drinks.

Marco opens by saying the invention of the atomic bomb is incompatible with the human species. It is one thing to build an arsenal – to hold stronger, more effective weaponry compared to an adversary – but it is an altogether other thing to create a weapon that goes beyond the rules of war. The atomic bomb is no different than a concentration camp.

The people of Hiroshima are surrounded by things of beauty, of a city rebuilt. But the slightest reminder of the past turns the world ugly. Hiroshima was destroyed because the world had nowhere else to search for peace. The aftermath does not go away. The rebuild is merely a reminder that in some other place the world is building its arsenal, in the hope to unleash future horrors. And it may choose to destroy all of humanity the next time.

No one person should ever have the right to make such decisions and inflict so much harm in the world. The people that roam the streets of Hiroshima have no right to reflect on the cruelty of the world. And the world has no right to open the debate about when might be the right time to use nuclear weapons.

And then suddenly a mushroom cloud, swirling with various kinds of rainbow configurations, appears in the sky. Some observers say they had never seen the shades of red and violet that appeared.

Hana argues that this gun is better than that one. Or this tank has better strength than their opponents. The nuclear arsenal does not have an adversary. It is not trying to battle per se, it is merely trying to destroy its enemy.

Trench warfare sounds acceptable, naval wars look impressive, even flyover bombardments have a touch of class.

Martin is from New Haven, a couple of hours north of NYC. He wears wide pants that can be described as skater pants. He finds half a dozen pairs at a flea market in New Haven, and then spends the next four years shoplifting for a living.

He met his girlfriend, Anh, who is Vietnamese, at the fryers when they worked at Wendy's. They also took a geography class together at the local high school.

Three years have passed since then. Two abortions later (one abortion was consecrated with the morning after pill that Martin claims does not count as a traditional abortion), and the two constantly bicker over the monthly four video game rentals from Video. Or else, they will bicker about whether one or both of them will go to Williamsburg and visit Neddy, Anh's brother, a tat artist (he attended twenty-seven conventions last year and made almost one million dollars).

The immediacy of their breakup was a shock to their system.

Martin got wasted on crystal meth and he cried for four days straight.

Later, they met at the hospital, while they were on suicide watch. Miraculously, each ventured from the hospital in different directions, and they've been relatively normal ever since.

The crystal meth experience has shown its full effect on Martin, and then some. His experience was not unlike the TV commercials back in the USA, prompted by Nancy Reagan's War on Drugs campaign, which inspired heaps of wannabe filmmakers, all based on the image of a fried egg: this is your brain on drugs.

Martin is a genuinely nice person. But he is overly confident, and this makes him appear rather obnoxious. In the tenth grade, he attended a Yale party. He entered the house and went to the fridge and discovered several levels of beer. He had never seen a fridge so full of beer in his whole life. He politely grabbed a beer, opened it, and entered the living room.

The party was just starting. There were lots of young Yalies who wore silky blouses and tights, the young men wore tees or button-down, collar shirts.

Eventually, a rather clever dope dealer from the neighborhood, Arnie, who had ingratiated himself into Stuart's life, noticed the out of place Martin and approached him.

Soon, they were swapping ideas about how Martin

found the party, and how he decided to take a beer from the fridge. Jake, who hosted the party, had no problem with Martin attending the party; however, Lucas, who had recently begun to take life a little too seriously, was quite upset by the interruption, and decided to put Martin out on his ear. Arnie tried to change Lucas's mind, but it was too late, and Martin was dragged through the house and tossed out of the door.

As commonplace and tame as they sound, these kinds of experiences have turned Martin into a rather topsy-turvy character.

He is not your typical American who eats orange cheese and wears black tees with knockoff pics of Robbie Knievel on the back. Or who admires their President. Martin is neither impressed with America, nor interested in pursuing its meaning. He is only interested in avoiding confrontations like he used to have at the 7-Eleven Slurpee area for an untold number of things, and hopefully finding a girlfriend someday.

Martin is such an enigmatic figure that one feels naturally obligated to take an interest in his life. If one did not pry or, at the very least, converse with the young American, one would appear a little cold. And cold is not the impression that Marco wants to create while he is in Japan. Indeed, befriending someone like Martin might boost his image considerably.

He wears a sign around his neck that says: "I travel around the world, and sleep in hostels, and work at menial jobs just to stay above the water. At least try and show me a little bit of respect."

Marco sees Martin as yet another proficient Japanese-speaking Western male who he has to try and mimic.

Curiously (this is where the two men have a meeting of minds), both Marco and Martin cannot come clean about why they like speaking to the other person so much.

"Are you American?"

"Yes. But that's not my real name, you can call me 'Martin'."

Marco fails to get the joke. And it is a rather insulting feeling to have when, Marco admits, he tends to struggle greatly at the best of times. Suddenly, they feel like old mates; as though they had been speaking English back in New Haven for the last twenty years.

They chat for over thirty minutes. And not once during that time does Marco return to Hana. Marco sees her lying on the lawn, and they send over hand gestures, saying I will be five more minutes.

Their conversations range from sports, to Rome, to Europe, and they even mention sex. Martin admits that he is uncomfortable talking about sex with another man. He claims that his ex has somehow ruined his memories of sex. But he does admit most Americans would be thrilled to engage him in all sorts of racy sexual talk.

"I'm just not the one to talk to about this stuff."

It is a rather awkward moment for the two men. However, they acknowledge that Martin has the right to say as he likes, but it did sound a touch incredulous given they've opened up so much already.

Marco looks at Hana, sunbathing, and naturally objectifies her beauty as much as he can, before Martin decides to change the subject. The two men spend a moment looking at the different Hiroshima monuments. And Martin falters for a moment, thinking they are two good ol' boys from back home, but then he stops dead in his tracks. And Martin finally accepts they have become friends.

"This is a very sacred place, you know."

"I know, I am here with my girlfriend…"

"Because I caused this destruction." Martin is aghast at his own comment. But holds a serious expression.

"Well, not you personally."

"Well, my grandparents opposed the war. Which in turn made our government very nervous, because they feared the Nazis would attack us. And if we didn't defend ourselves, we were goners. Our parents decided to take a hard line. And drop the bomb. And I think the pacifists had a lot to do with triggering this kind of reaction from our government."

They could not be further apart. Indeed, Martin, who suddenly sees the error of his way, has somehow internalized the history of Hiroshima. And Marco appears quite open to the proposition, which, in fact, works very well as a building block for Marco and Hana's own private theories about the war. But Martin quickly tries to collect his thoughts and end the conversation.

Marco lurches towards Hana, who is sitting in the sun. She points towards an orange soda station and wants to buy a drink. Marco directs an angry stare at Martin, because Martin has crossed the line and said something no decent or reasonable man would say to another person. And just when he is about to ask for an apology, Martin rubs his eyes and smiles mischievously, as though the two men have a meeting of minds.

"I still cannot come to the conclusion that it is your grandparents' fault."

"Actually, Grandpa was Mennonite, and he was pacifist, and he opposed the war, but Grandma was very militaristic, and she supported the war. She has told me that many times."

"I see."

"You must understand, no persons in the United States during World War II were pacifists."

"I don't quite get that?" Marco peers over at Hana, who replies with a gentle wave.

"Pacifism would not have helped us very much. We needed to be militaristic in order to defend ourselves."

"Of course, you did. Of course."

Suddenly, a cloud passes in front of the sun. And Martin feels ashamed that he would say such things to another person. And he knows it is just because he is away from home. Or else, he is acting out because Marco's English is not very good, and he can take risks in their conversations.

A silence hovers in the air. Neither man knows how to end their meeting. And then it dawns on them – at the same time: they will loosen up. And they recognize in each other that neither one was going to be special in the world, say, work in politics or teach in university, and so each lets down his guard. And neither of their Presidents, Mattarella or Biden respectively, represent characters they aspire to mimic. They smile at each other. They conspire how they could deepen their friendship. Marco turns and looks anxiously at Hana. Or else Martin reads something on CNN on his phone, and acts as though the story sounds funny, and peeks up at Marco to see if he still wants to chat. And both men decide they will renew their conversation. But, strangely, neither one knows what that means. They are, in fact, caught in a rather complex situation, and neither one knows how to escape.

"What's the deal with the Japanese girlfriend?"

"Oh, Hana?"

"She is very beautiful."

Martin waited for a response, but perhaps he didn't speak clearly enough.

"Don't be so modest, she really is quite beautiful."

"Oh, I know."

Martin could sense that Marco wanted to change the direction of their conversation.

"I just can't get over that we're here together."

"What do you mean?"

"This place is so sacred. And I don't know if you know this, but as an American, I actually feel a little strange being here. Do you think I should feel like that?"

They search for new ways of communicating to each other. They are becoming protective of the other person. And they insist on venturing forward as friends.

"This might sound strange to say, but I don't think that many Americans think about these kinds of things."

"I don't think most Europeans do either."

"I wonder what the Japanese think?"

"What's the old expression? If a tree falls in a forest and no one is around to hear it... when an atomic bomb falls, and no one is around to hear it...does it really make a sound?"

"Oh, rubbish, history knows very well what happened. I know what happened."

Hana stands beside Marco. She grabs his arm and puts it over her shoulder. Martin cannot take his eyes off her. And Hana feels the weight of Martin's stare. This is how Marco wants it. He does not want any divisions with his new friend. And even though it might appear a little forward, there is something refreshing in how Martin coolly disregards the couple's status. It wears off, and finally, by some exterior force, Martin reaches his hand towards Hana. In a quasi-British-American manner, Martin feigns indignation about the situation and offers a polite handshake in the hope that they might return to a shared common ground.

Hana instead reaches over towards Martin and kisses him on both cheeks.

"Nice to meet you!"

The glossy, bright-colored pamphlet describes Hiroshima as a form of dark tourism, or battlefield tourism. It is one among many such places around the world, including the western African slave ports, or the concentration camps in Germany and across Europe.

As sombre as the pamphlet appears, it also names a great place to enjoy a cappuccino and where to find the nearest bathrooms. The brochure does not mention Plato, or walking on the moon, or Dr. Martin Luther King. It wants to remember the mushroom cloud. Despite the past, today many want to celebrate this place, and treats make the whole process much more enjoyable.

It is the Boulder sky, Hana keeps repeating, and Marco appears aloof from her words. Marco looks over the motel room, and he knows his responsibilities for tomorrow. He must take the memory chip and return to the hotel room and upload the data on his laptop.

Suddenly, he has doubts. His partner – the cool, unproven, sultry, Japanese vixen – is having second thoughts. She sits in the bathtub and sings and shaves her legs. Marco's appraisement about the job is in shatters.

There is never any point for players to become friends on a job. The goal is to maximise the profits for both groups. Besides, players who mix tend to create jealousies.

The neon lights, the florescent signage, the deafening sounds of technology are a quick reminder to anyone about Japan's vast differences from the rest of Asia.

A large group of tourists take over the shop. The tour guide speaks through a loudspeaker. The aisles, islands, glass counters, and spinning shelves are ransacked and before not very long the best deals are found and erased from existence.

Vexed stares from the group take over the shop. And slowly the race to make last minute purchases is on everyone's mind. And even the economy, the mounds of merchandise, the crash, run-for-the-hills sales can't compete against the buyers' appetites.

The island of electronics is like the centerpiece of some important wedding. Marco stands frozen in front of a small table of electronics. One of the items comprises a Christmas ornament with a mini-TV set inside the delicate glass. It includes a time lapse which you can modify. Or else, there is the fishbowl that is covered in a digital screen which, from all angles, makes you think it is an actual fishbowl with real fish.

A salesman approaches Marco.

"You made a nice choice, even though it is summer."

"I love all this stuff that you have."

"Yeah, the home of electronics is our motto."

Marco has no idea what the salesman is actually trying to say.

"You can't find any of these things in Rome."

"No?"

Shoes are left at the door, colorful bags remain half-filled with mall purchases, candies in lacquer bowls, a cool face cloth lies over some spilled Diet Dr. Pepper.

Marco lies half asleep on the thickly upholstered chair, and awkwardly reaches down and gives Sota a few scratches behind the ear. He considers the World War II memorabilia on the bookshelf and notices Hana speaking in hushed tones to her Aunt Naomi on her iPhone.

The comforter is neatly tucked under each corner, the sheet is neatly folded over, almost too tightly, but a pristine pillow rests on the fold. Near the window rests a table and leather swivel. He will enter the sun-warmed room tomorrow, sit at the desk, and upload the information. He will exit the room, the twisty carpet, and shake hands with players from Moscow.

They go downstairs and notice the two sisters, Midori and Naomi, chatting away. Hana pulls Marco back upstairs. She wants Marco to learn more about her Aunt Naomi before she makes introductions. Naomi is eccentric and full of stories. She is a social butterfly with an impeccable reputation. She is ultra-religious, yet it remains a taboo topic. And she lives for her family, and nothing else. Never married, as it would be wasteful and probably anti-religious to marry a man anyway. Marco breaks into a smile.

The back yard is tiny. And five adults sitting around a small, wobbly table, and Sota meandering, makes it feel cramped. But the warmth and companionship amongst the group pushes aside any possibility of inconvenience.

Naomi opens her purse and removes a bottle of *Kikori* Rice Whiskey. She offers Marco a shot, and, after looking at Hana and her parents for permission, takes a rather impressive swig, making everyone at the table laugh.

There is a major difference between making eye contact and then bringing a drink up to your mouth and adding to the conversation. He can start to study Japanese in earnest, but even then, his answers will always sound scripted.

The key to a successful transition from the job to normal life is family.

He swears off being an outsider. The forces of a foreign language are upon him, and he has already become so close to Hana. He smiles. The table knows all too well the challenges of the language barrier. Midori brushes Hana's long, black hair out of her eyes, off her face, and silently communicates to her daughter the hardships that sometimes arise in a relationship.

The snip of time that Naomi spends noticing Marco is quickly erased, as Midori talks in a faster clip, making it seem impossible for someone to learn Japanese as a second language.

She turns to Marco, and uses her hands very rigidly, and then cries with laughter at trying to answer questions. And no one feels burdened with their inability to speak.

Techniques have been developed to read between the lines. They speak a few lines of English. They find some happy common ground. And now they laugh at their lack of English skills.

Naomi lowers her head. And then announces her best friend, Kanako, was recently raped.

Marco shakes his head in consternation. Instantly, he realizes this is the conversation he was warned about earlier. Hana puts her hand on Marco's thigh, and they share a moment together. And it is beautiful. And Naomi continues her anecdote, sometimes stopping between tears, always looking directly at Marco.

"Rape is not nice!"

Marco wonders why this happens so suddenly.

There is considerable discomfort, and even some panic to try and compose oneself. They understand each other as a group. And it feels genuine. Natural. And no sooner had this happened than Naomi and Midori are in deep conversation and Marco is left on his own.

There is much hooting and hollering as a couple of techies perform a break-dance routine. They try and pull Hana onto the dance floor, but she declines. And then Marco politely hangs his arm against her sleeveless shoulder.

Emergencies are good because they deflect attention from the domestic habits, which, in fact, are not real. In other words, emergencies create an overwhelming calm that is good for the whole operation.

First, Midori applies small karate chops, and then she taps her hands lightly on Naomi's neck. The massage works to loosen the muscles and tension that Naomi feels in her neck.

Everyone feels overpowered by the situation. The two men make eye contact, and they are man enough to refute what they are hearing. In other words, neither one is capable of doing such an act to a woman. And everyone is comforted that they are together to consider these thoughts.

They must act brave, for this is not some scheduled meeting with the Chief Inspector, with contemplative DSs sitting at a big table, thinking of ways to crack a case.

The highlights of the job must turn invisible. The job must feel like fiction. Make the job part of the world you see at the movies. Think of yourself as having been tossed out of your job, and yet you still have to pay the rent. The domestic life is your second chance.

It is, everyone admits, a little over the top, brazen, and infuriating, but they have a moment of silence to deliberate about such evil in the world, and everyone feels a little cleansed by the process.

Marco refers to Google Maps. They plan a two-day trip to Mount Hiruzen to walk along the ridgeline. The drive takes approximately two hours and spans almost the entire width of the country.

On the northwestern side of the small island lies the Sea of Japan. South Korea is a stone's throw away, and North Korea and China a little further down the street. The proximity of these two mighty countries will make anyone tremble and certainly justifies a civic responsibility like no other. However, the opposite stretch of the country, the eastern coast, faces the awesome Pacific Ocean. The vastness of the great ocean puts everything into perspective. Suddenly, Japan is a small island, isolated, vulnerable to the whims of a horrendous body of water.

It was once part of mainland China and Korea. Consequently, there remains an affinity towards these countries even though there are so many cultural and political differences.

The most striking aspect of Japan is its enormous population, at one hundred and thirty million. More than eighty per cent live in a localized area.

They pack light for their weekend adventure: a two-man tent, a sleeping bag and blanket, two soft pillows, and a cooler full of food. They listen to classic rock like Brian Adams, Madonna, and Bruce Springsteen. Hana likes to lower the window and scream "Bruce" as loud as she possibly can. Marco tries his best to keep up, but mostly he keeps an eye on the steering wheel in case Hana decides to go over the top while she looks outside and screams "Bruce".

Marco goes over to the row of garbage cans. He tries to read the Kenji characters underneath. A couple get out of a VW van and go towards Marco. The medium built man with bull legs approaches Marco and stops right in front of him.

There is an unmistakable atmosphere of danger. The man with the knit skull cap twiddles his lanky fingers near his biceps, and then lurches over to a pocket, rips the Velcro, and removes a spaghetti handful of colorful joints. He takes his other hand, a well-disciplined robotic arm, grabs a joint and drops it into Marco's hand.

"This will really mess you up, so be careful."

Mount Hiruzen is about a twenty-five-mile hike from start to finish. It is hard, grassy ground, with a clearly defined path. From the ridgeline the views are panoramic, and quickly justify the choice to go on the walk. This is not the Italian Alps, or the Rocky Mountains, which the couple explored during their trip to Boulder, which included one hundred-foot pines, and soggy trails, jade lakes, and disassembled hunting cabins (full of discarded kerosene cans transformed into mini-barbecues to cook hotdogs).

The hike is challenging and life-affirming. A signpost on the path gives directions to the next stopping point. The sloping path, the crest of the rolling hills, feels like a struggle with every step. It is covered in discarded flowers, or else little flags from Japan. Someone has even put a small dish of sake for visitors to sip.

They reach a good spot and decide to put up the tent. Hana takes some water from the water bottle and dampens her bandana. They appear more athletic than they should, given that neither one has gone hiking before. As they enter the tent, Hana lightly taps Marco's jacket pocket for the joint.

Marco lights the joint and has taken several hits when they hear something from outside.

A police officer in a pristine police uniform and with a shiny bike approaches Marco's tent.

The police officer speaks to Marco while Marco remains inside the tent.

"What is that smell?"

"I don't know."

"Is that cannabis?"

"No."

Marco eats the joint.

Marco exits the tent.

The two men speak for several minutes about Marco's background. Marco explains they have just come back from Boulder.

"I used to live in Boulder." The police officer raises the handlebars of his bike, indicating he is all set to leave.

"Get out!"

Hana kicks Marco in the shin.

"We met in Boulder."

The officer looks across the mountain range, and then comes back to the couple.

"The Colorado Avalanche are my favorite team."

"OK."

The police officer pokes his nose into the side of Marco's face.

"You better not die on that joint you swallowed. Because it will be me that has to fill out the form."

They finish a bottle of wine. Marco signals he has reached his limit, and Hana adds they have just begun. She crawls out of the tent into the starry night, zip, and returns with another bottle.

They are free to act as they like. And they are sensitive to each other. They test their strengths, their likes and dislikes. Each craves the other's attention; each wants nothing more than to be with the other.

They wonder when they can wear a face that says they are angry about the war. And that man wears an evil face. They know that. They want to wear the mask of their family members who died. The mask is eternally revengeful – regardless of which side of the war one finds oneself on.

It does not matter that they have destroyed the tent. It does not matter that Marco has popped his head outside and looked up at the stars while he makes love. He sees the glow of a small campfire perhaps two or three hundred yards away. It does not matter that they both laugh at thinking they have become designers for The North Face, and they are designing the most prized outfit for a Paris runway show. And then the sex stops. They smile with clenched teeth and say "I love you".

She walks a little distance before she comes to a little bluff. The moonlight shines a glossy layer on the diverse terrain. She hears the sounds of laughter. The hissing laughs fade away as she trudges along. She finds the tent.

A naked Hana inspecting the outdoors is as close to feminism as Marco wants to get. She continues to stand at the door of the tent and sips her morning coffee. She gets dressed. They finish the second half of the ridge in record time. When they arrive at the car, Marco throws his knapsack on the wet ground, goes down on one knee, and proposes. Hana begins to cry. She begins a light jog down the road towards the main highway. She zigzags across the road. He sprints towards her, and then he takes her in his arms, and they fall over onto the side of the rocky road. She cups Marco's face in her trembling hands and says "I do."

The next morning, Hana lies in her bed and repeats "Boulder" several times out loud. She sees her phone on the expensive carpet, vibrating. And now she is late. She must go to the bank and meet the other contacts.

Families have a way of destroying the unit.

They decide to lie down and rest. They awaken half an hour later, Hana rubs Marco's stomach and calls him her teddy bear. They decide to get back on the road. Shortly after, they go to a Burger King drive-thru, and they feel much better than before.

They reflect on their trip to Hiroshima. They turn wise and confessional. Hana admits it is strange that her family once supported Hirohito. The next generation of Japanese switched their allegiance. And yet she wonders how that is possible. Never mind the Japanese surrender in 1945. Or else Japan signing the San Francisco Peace Treaty in 1951. She finds it hard to fathom how her parents were able to suddenly accept that their parents lost the war. Especially after so many Japanese lives had been lost.

There is always a loser in war. For example, the Ottoman Empire, which once reigned over central and southern Europe. The Germans, of course, are the greatest losers, losing World War I and World War II.

Her family is at peace with their vision of the future.

An atomic bomb has landed. Suddenly, city officials in Hiroshima are fielding calls from nosey American developers who want to build palatial hotels for lefty Americans to spend heaps of money and ask for forgiveness when they visit months later.

Hana's family recognize the American tourists, who have big mugs, and wear Reeboks and act apologetic, but still insist on saying things like "how much should I tip?"

One shop owner, who owns a hardware store, puts an American flag in front of his shop, mostly as a social experiment. And suddenly, he is inundated with picture requests. He sets it up like a picture booth for tourists, and makes a pretty dime every day, even though locals find his choice to hoist the flag tacky.

And once more Hana tries to understand what really happened. She understands the empirical rants. She knows about all the events, the concentration camps. She only questions her family's connection to the war.

Where were they? How many of her family died during the war? How many of her extended family and friends died? Or else where do all these people go once a war ends?

There is always a loser in war, she repeats.

The outside world sometimes appears invisible. It is a mixture of ignorance, apathy, and the ways they have been nurtured (in the colloquial, contemporary, psychological verbiage, to have already been radicalized to perform crime).

For a moment, the outside world feels invisible. Or else the images of a victory parade down Broadway in NYC are invisible in her mind. Even the victor has disappeared. All that remains are the empty expressions of friends and relatives. And suddenly there is no further discussion about the war. There are no rationalizations. Instead, it is a new day, and nothing more.

They return to the car. Hana kisses Marco on the side of the neck. She asks him if it bothers him that they discuss the war. Marco admits they are saying things that he always wanted to talk about.

Let's say you fall in love. And it does happen. Every topic under the sun is useful. We ask that you explore love's gifts, the joys of unification, and by all means share in each other's secrets. Your next job will be grateful that you two have met.

The Americans' choice to use the atomic bomb remains a storm in their minds.

Perhaps they should be talking about something else. Or else, are they square for bringing up the past, and turning the page about something, and choosing to talk about the past some more?

History abounds with reason. But their discussion about Hiroshima gives a different perspective. The historical process is unfolding before their eyes. And they are content to judge the war more and more as time goes by.

They have left a dark place: the land of murder. No shelter is safe. A human being was never considered important in the place they just visited. It was targeted to be erased, in order to shift thinking, to make someone say "we give up". And yet the space itself is not rememberable. And it is unlikely that Hiroshima will ever be reachable.

They enter Tokyo. She points at all the different places, like the Suzuki plant where her father works. She wants to refresh Marco about a world that is alive, that strives to go forward. Marco is moved by all the sights and cannot get how Hana has so easily conquered their dark past by showing off her city. Her city has captured the spirit of going forward. But truthfully, Hana is still numb by Marco's proposal. She grips his leg as they drive. And now every turn becomes more intense in anticipation of seeing her mother and telling her the exciting news. Marco falls out of sight.

The parents' reaction is dull and uneventful. Hirato opens a bottle of wine. These are still just kids in his eyes (he has no time to consult with his wife about his real feelings). Midori places her wine glass on the table, and rushes off into the other room, giving the impression she is already behind in the wedding plans. The Sunday billiard game is still the most important thing on the schedule. Hirato shakes Marco's hand with some added frenzy.

They watch Whitney on Netflix. Tsumugi says she

intends to get very drunk at their wedding.

Marco gets the answering machine. Serena calls him back, but before he can share the big news, she interjects that she is with friends at Italia Café. Finally, Serena comes on the line, and he blurts out that he is engaged.

"To do what?"

She has sucked all the energy out of the room. They are no longer friends. He tells his mother he wishes she was more like Midori. Hana grabs the phone and yells "hi, Mom!"

Domestic troubles will help cover you in ways you cannot possibly fathom. A mother cursing a son or daughter is far more strategic in the layering process than anything else. We only kill for money. And our money needs to be protected from real events.

The Book is available in PDF. In order to receive a copy, you must first fill out an online form.

The Book is about two hundred pages. It includes a glossary of terms and a timeline which shows the major heists for the past two hundred years. The heists section is considered the most prized section.

The Book opens with a little essay on the perfect crime. I shall include a copy of the essay here:

Does a perfect crime exist? For some, it is an irrational question. That is to say, for the moralists of the world, (those who oppose the criminal lifestyle) any answer will appear like a contradiction in terms. Obviously, those of us in the crime business think differently. But notice that we are not giving carte blanche to just anyone to commit a crime, and then shower them in praise for what they have accomplished.

We don't honour the martyr, the mass murderer, or revenge killings. The Book recognizes crimes that somehow enhance the idea of criminality in such a way that future generations of criminals can look forward to a life of crime.

For example, it might be a series of bank robberies. You might have a gangster who robs a bank and then lives off his assets for a few years. And then, one day, he realizes he is running out of money. He decides to go out and rob another bank. He might do this five or six times, until he is wealthy enough to retire.

This gangster only got out of bed five times, and now he is set for life. And he can take pride in knowing that he knocked off a bank. It takes a lot of focus and physical strength to enter a branch, go up to the teller, and demand money. But it only takes one suspicious type to destroy their world. This type of gangster lives with a lot of anxiety, which takes away from the glam. (There are exceptions, of course, but generally speaking that is the take on the matter).

Another perfect crime might be online fraud. But online fraud usually involves a lot of people, and it begins to feel like we're running a company, and so we tend to avoid it.

And then there are the art heists. We have seen jobs where they've entered a museum, avoided all sorts of security, and fled with some priceless works of art. We like these jobs, because they tend to idealize the criminal element.

Of course, we cannot forget the counterfeit jobs.

The problem with counterfeit jobs, however, is that they can sometimes hurt you in the back end. For example, if we put money on the streets, and we get involved in our own engagements, and suddenly the feds pull the rug from under our feet, we've lost the dough we layered into the system. Counterfeit is a tough racket, and you never want to die on your own supply!

The perfect crime tends to always involve gold, silver, or gems of some sort.

New York City has the Diamond District. And we've squeezed this world better than most. The Diamond District holds all the riches we will someday possess. It's like a weighing station, before the goods are dispatched around the world. Indeed, we keep tabs on the Diamond District, just like someone might read the New York Times and follow the stock market.

Recall the French philosopher, Michel Foucault, who studied mental health institutions and the prison system, and came up with all sorts of sociological theories. The infrastructure of the institutions themselves have an impact on a person's mind. Or how these institutions impact society over time. At any rate, I won't go into detail, but the truth of the matter is, there is a lot of run off in our business, and those are places where the runoff end up. But what Foucault misses, and what a lot of the academics who follow on his coattails overlook, is the religious element.

In other words, we acknowledge that prisons and mental health institutions exist in droves, and on the periphery of life they are a nuisance. But the almighty dream of a perfect crime and the impulse of the criminal have nothing to do with these places. Most good criminals are seeking pure perfection.

Foucault has his eye too focussed on history, in the past, whereas the criminal looks towards the future. At the next best thing, such as gems.

Gems have meaning for everyone: religious or non-religious, for the criminal or non-criminal alike. The Royals look forward to wearing their jewels, men and women look fancy when they wear their jewels. Some things will never change.

The idea of making enough money to buy your girlfriend a nice bracelet will never go out of fashion. This is what makes the world turn. And this is where we feel most comfortable, namely controlling these kinds of emotions in people. And maybe, every once in a while, someone will look up and notice a diamond is missing from the jewelry box. It might not mean very much right away, but ultimately these are the little events that the criminal has masterminded to capture. And collectively these kinds of events are what make the perfect crime.

The reason why the Book remains useful is because it reflects things that are happening in the world today. It remains a paradox, for the crimes themselves are unforgiveable, and yet they offer players the rules of the game in which more glorious crimes can be committed.

We had a slew of contracts to work in Latin America. A lot of these contracts were generated from the CIA and FBI, but also a diverse range of political organizations, especially in Argentina, Peru, Chili, and Venezuela.

Some of our friends – some of the better-known Italian crime families – thought it was good business to get involved in politics. It turns out it was the wrong decision. To this day, you cannot mention Marilyn Monroe without someone saying something disrespectful towards hard-working Italian Americans. It is best to avoid the political and entertainment sectors as much as possible.

The strength of our organization is based on crime

and finding ways to make money any which way you can. We're never going to get our claws deep enough into politics to allow us to control everything we want absolutely. We have decided to stay out. Don't get me wrong, if an order comes up for an assassination, we're more than interested in putting in an offer. But it is no longer a priority like it was in the past. We are deliberating our business decision in this matter, and we will make final decisions as the future comes up.

The Book has become a huge hit with criminal groups all over the world. They can't get their hands off it. Every day we are inundated with requests. We've even been invited to give talks. Famous politicians with connections to the White House have offered us six figures for a dinner speech in Manhattan, which included two nights at Trump Tower, which is no kick in the pants.

We've had to turn down these kinds of offers to protect our image.

The thing to understand is that the Book is as essential to the history of crime as the colorful crimes themselves. Many people have inquired whether the Book gets in the way of committing crime? On the contrary, we are trying to teach you the right ways to commit a crime.

Be reminded, the Book promotes criminality. Please dispense with referring to your well-respected understanding of the criminal mind. We sublimate the negative stereotype and endorse the breathing criminal mind. Rather than picture the criminal inside a cramped cell or hiding, imagine that he has just paid his bill at the Ritz-Carleton. Or that he has donated some money to the gray nuns. Or that he has just mastered cracking a new kind of safe that is reputed to be uncrackable.

One time, we received a letter asking for the address

of some known bandit in Hawaii, who made off with a bag of loot. The family that was robbed put an impressive bounty on the thieves, but we didn't end up intervening and instead recommended they purchase a new security system.

The revenge game slowly disappears. The gangsters themselves prefer to come clean about their proclivities, for there is no money to be made in the revenge game.

It has been brought to our attention that the police have found copies of the Book. However, upon reading the outlandish stories, they instinctively dispute its authenticity.

Our writers, who write the summaries, are some of the finest mind's money can find. They tend to be philosophy dropouts from schools like New School for Social Research, Berkeley, and Oxford University. Every couple of years, we place a stool in a first-year class, and whoever stands out, we try and get their attention.

One of our writers works at a library in Scotland. He has several proofreaders who live in the USA, Canada, and two in India.

Let's say there is a dispute between two rival gangs regarding a street tax for drug trafficking. You can always refer to the Book and see how many deals have been made over a stretch of time in a specific area.

We do not claim our numbers are spot on, but they are better than anything you will find on the street. And the street criminal understands the importance of the Book. The street criminals will meet with our representatives regularly and square up any questions about any recent criminal activity.

Obviously, this leads to bloodshed and reprisals but, in fairness, our people think that spreading the right *information helps criminal organizations deal with real problems. Rather than work on innuendo and rumour, they can kill someone and say the Book has good information that so-and-so made this amount of money based on this deal. We are keeping things straight.*

In the end, the Book is a resource. The real winners are the players themselves, whether or not they decide to use the Book is at their own discretion.

Marco sits on the upstairs couch inside Hana's parents' house. He would much prefer to take an arm's length approach, like some of his friends have done with their parents (they see each other on special occasions, and at Sunday family dinners, of course), but Marco and Serena are beyond acquaintances. Marco has put them in a special place. And the closeness is beautiful and genuine, but at great sacrifice to their personal freedom. And neither one is willing to inquire what that means.

She spins. Her smile is so big she nearly falls over. And Marco is one with her.

"Yeah, you're making the biggest mistake of your life."

Marco stands up and goes over to the window.

"What?"

"If you think you are going to get married at your age, with no job, then you are being stupid."

"Forget that I called. And forget about the wedding. Because you are not invited anyway."

"Good."

He must return to Rome, and everyone will meet: "...and then we'll decide as a family if you are right for each other."

She is setting him up to say he is making the biggest

mistake of his life. Marco knows that nothing is ever easy with his mother.

Marco figures he is always doing his best, and his mother should give him more credit. On the other hand, he is blameworthy for some of life's mistakes, and some of these mistakes appear rather impressive…for example, a physical ailment preventing him from making the Napoli squad.

Marco watches as Hirato dispenses the miso. He is famous for his miso. In fact, each year, when he digs up one of the clay pots after the fermentation period, huge crowds attend. The neighbors line up, and hold Tupperware, *Shigaraki* ware, and *karatsu* ware, and sometimes the old-timers will come with a prepared dish, just to taste the miso right on the spot.

In Boulder, the bank teller doesn't appear very busy. One teller, slender in a slinky dress, sends a DM to her husband. The manager, who wears floods, a thick cotton shirt, and pink tie with a clip, struts with a coffee past the empty wickets. A nervous Hana enters the bank and walks nonchalantly to the closest wicket, skipping the line. The teller, an older man with gray whiskers, looks over-worked, and seems a little stinky from drinks with his sister the night before.

The money is brought out on a little cart. In one hundred-dollar bills, two million dollars amounts to twenty thousand bills. It is forty-three inches per ten thousand bundle, and so in total one needs a large duffle bag to hold all the money. The strap color differs depending on the denomination. Hana requests one hundred-dollar bills. The strap is mustard. The bills have the profile of Benjamin Franklin on one side, and on the flip, it shows a vignette of Independence Hall.

Hana kneels down beside the money, and sweeps her hand over the top, but she continues to stare at the teller, who acts a little jumpy by the exchange. And then Hana grabs a bundle, and brings it to her face, and rubs the bills lightly against her cheek. At this point, the teller has had enough and returns to his wicket.

The bank manager, meanwhile, remains beside Hana, but he does not react with dismissal towards the teller for leaving, and instead casually looks out the front doors, to make sure the security guard is ready for when Hana decides to leave.

The security guard, who thinks everyone is acting far too casually, is sidetracked to the time he was at the movies, and he has just put down his popcorn and drink. The moment of putting down his popcorn and returning to the movie is the same feeling he has while noticing the bank manager, and then looking over at Hana.

Hirato stands in the backyard of their home in Tokyo. Under the flickering back yard light, he dispenses some of the miso into another clay pot. He has repeated this process countless times. He appears like a horticultural chef, someone committed to demonstrating good in their community.

Hirato is partaking in the act of giving an *oseibo* gift, where one is not expecting anything in return.

The sharing of miso builds a sense of pride in Hirato. He shares his miso as a way to say "thanks" to his neighbors for being his friends. There is no pretext, nor any pretensions for that matter (if someone prefers their own miso, Hirato is OK with that), but ultimately it is the act of sharing that Hirato is interested in. He helps his neighbors to understand that he is being genuine when he reaches out.

If someone were to question his cooking habits, the conversation would end. Or else Midori would come around and interrupt the ruckus and say that he makes miso because he likes the attention or because he is a social butterfly at heart.

"How was Hiroshima?"

And suddenly they search each other's eyes. And yet neither one ventures to tell the other person what they really think. It remains sealed. But it is this kind of silence that preoccupies them even more.

The question hovers. Marco lets Hana answer. And in her speedy Japanese manner, she controls the conversation with her father.

"Hiroshima reminds me of the expressions I see on the faces of people I meet in Rome."

"Oh."

It erupts into a shouting match which has repeated itself over and over many times before. Hirato recalls the stories handed down from his grandfather and father. And Midori, who is familiar with all of these stories, ends up correcting Hirato, which tends to escalate things even further.

Midori cries at the revelation. And in some angelic voice she somehow places blame on Hirato's dad for being in the wrong place at the wrong time. And Hirato, who always cries at the memory of his father, agrees with his wife, and even manages a few chuckles, about the absurdity of their conversation.

But Hirato has his own ideas of the past. And no matter what anyone else says, especially his only daughter, he holds to his own ideas.

Marco's answer is neither poetic, profound, nor resembling a young man reaching out to his father-in-law. All those marks are earned. But rather, Hiroshima remains too fresh for Hirato. Indeed, the event recapitulates, or is churning like some constantly altering pathogen, at any time it is an act of war, and then an episode difficult to defend, and then suddenly it becomes a part of western history. Or else there are stories wrapped in American propaganda. A reversal stereotype game plays out. That is, Westerners tend to stereotype Asians for their touristy manner – camera-toting, big group assemblies – and suddenly the tables have turned.

First, it was shrouded in silence. Today, it marks a distraction for foreigners. It has assumed a joke for many Japanese.

They are like strangers as they walk towards the Sogenji Temple. Not in a despairing way, like when you attend a party with someone, and you ingratiate yourself into a new crowd, ignoring your companion. Alas, you have got rid of the clingy feeling.

Hana knows the history behind the Buddhist temple, and she is building on her knowledge. Marco admires the architecture or else the pine trees, the fresh air. Marco grew up in Esquilino, a poor section of Rome, and they never ventured outside the neighborhood. Family tended to come to Rome for visits. And besides, playing soccer, always on the pitch, made them feel like they were always in the outdoors.

One day it is a personal anecdote, the next day it is part of world history.

Hana appears even more radiant, for she is neither interested in Buddhism, nor understands the sales pitch about this place. And sure enough, Hana and Marco stand out – the lovely Japanese woman and handsome European man. Soon, Hana is being chatted up by one of the regulars. She is invited to a meet and greet on Saturday at 9 a.m. Marco distances himself from their talk with the same kind of indifference that Hana shows when they first approach the temple.

The frustrations are superficial: there are no lavatories or vending machines. The temple assumes a more powerful meaning. They stand apart from one another, and act like they are in a music video. Hana walks across the granulated ground like she is a fashion model. Or she passes Marco and says something in Japanese. Marco goes up to Hana and speaks Italian. Hana begins to laugh. Even the Buddhists who have arrived early find their game amusing. The temple no longer represents a place of expanding one's consciousness, tranquility, or anything Japanese for that matter. It is a place of experimentation.

There is only one project greater than the job, and that is religion. It is the institution that stands in our path. It makes a mockery of our work and lifestyle. The unit has opted to stop working with religious institutions. That being said, if you find there is some way to work with a specific religion, say, some rich church, and it promises a rich pay day, then give us a call on the 1-800 number and we can discuss what your options are.

Marco recalls a time during his youth, a school trip to Paris. And the power of the Catholic church at that time. And how pompous the Catholic church appeared.

He examines the layout of the temple more closely. He imagines himself as a Buddhist; or else, he wears the costume of a Buddhist monk. The different colored robes abound around him, multi-shades of orange and saffron.

She is not about to abandon her past for Marco's benefit. She resents that she would sacrifice the truth of this place for some gains in their relationship. Hana uses silence to show respect, and she silently gives this place back to itself. Marco recognizes her behaviour, but he is still keen to have more fun. They smile and kiss as they approach the car. Their faces rub against each other and soon, their minds race about making love.

Hana pulls over to an ATM and takes out some money. Next, the couple enter the pharmacy and buy Q-tips. The trance of the pharmacy is an even more powerful experience than the Shinto Temple. And the irony is not lost on Hana; she needles out any sales she can find.

He likes the city and people. There is a tremendous warmth amongst the population, and he could eventually find his niche. But he is not ready to settle into thinking like that.

Marco is reminded he is not at home, and the visit is creating tension on their relationship. Hana is committed to their life together, and Marco is also eager to begin their life, but it doesn't appear to want to manifest in Japan. The future feels like it is on hold. Marco begins to think more and more about Italy. Hana's parents want the young couple to live as a couple in Japan. A deep wonder emerges for everyone inside the modest sized home.

Another tension lies in the fact that Marco is Roman Catholic. The most conservative theologian would politely ask Marco to loosen up. And he is not the least bit curious about this facet of his personality. He is incorrigible about his faith. He attends mass on Sundays when he finds the time.

Indeed, Marco discerns the only way he has come to terms with his father's (Frank's) passing is by reading the Bible. He says that without certain passages, he could never have survived the period of mourning, which he says lasted about three months. Serena sometimes asks him "why only three months?" and he replies, "it sounds like a good enough number."

His mind travelling back to Paris, Marco recalls looking at the gargoyles, at the dome interior, at the stained-glass window. He needed some air. He walked over to the barricade that overlooks Paris, and suddenly a deep sense of religiosity swept through his body. He looked back at the imposing Montmartre. At that moment, he decided that he would build religion into his life, and it would exceed the grandeur of this place.

Football was alive and well in Paris, for the French, as everyone knows, are a great football nation. The sisters accompanying the school group were tired after a disastrous visit to the Louvre. The children were given free rein to play football at Tuileries Garden.

The fact that Hana is not Catholic arouses little interest for Marco. Quite the contrary, they see their relationship as resting on several pressure points, and they endeavor to become stronger in the shape of their faith, together. They are excited by the prospect of shaping Catholicism to their own likes and dislikes.

Their conversations often turn humorous, because Marco is in the habit of always digressing whenever they mention God. He likes to interrupt these lofty conversations by saying he doesn't have all the answers. Or his particular favorite: "only God knows about such things." Hana remains the procrastinator. She continues to heckle Marco to come clean about his true feelings. And the more she heckles, the more he dodges her questions. They succeed in talking about God together.

Please do not make out that you are a know it all. Religion is murky territory at the best of times, and we know that, for some, it holds a bad reputation all of the time. If you have questions, just call the 1-800 number.

Catholicism has not penetrated the Japanese culture like it has in many other countries. It remains a mystery to the Japanese.

Not that Christendom did not try and penetrate Japan, but the Japanese forbade its expansion. Instead, the Japanese choose Shintoism. The term "Shinto" means "way of the Gods". There are references to Shinto that predate the history of Japan. When a new religion, like Catholicism, comes into the fold, and given it originated in the West, the instinct is to put it down as something from the outside.

A small tree has meaning. A path has meaning. A stream of water has meaning. Collectively these things breathe life into the world.

The tree represents life, and its growth is contingent on a great many factors. Depending on the setting, man might be the main source of preserving the life of the tree. That is the sense in which Hana's family embraces Shinto and philosophy. This sense of caring helps everyone to be kinder to each other, more than ever before.

However, Marco is offering a brand of religion that is unique. It is an accumulation of all his knowledge up to this point in his life. And the participation of someone else makes the journey even more exciting.

Hirato sits in the backyard and smokes a cigar. Sota tries to take the cigar from his mouth. Hana sunbathes under the hot sun. The phone rings. The house wreaks with drama.

Kanako is able to identify the man but refuses to say anything to the police because she knows him from the neighborhood. Midori shrieks at the news and speaks despairingly about Kanako's decision not to go to the police. Hana refuses to enter the debate.

Indeed, Hana takes a strong "whodunnit" take on the situation, and offers a sideways look, as if to say that Kanako had no right to walk away from pressing charges just because she happened to know the man. Naomi decides not to defend her friend.

It is a conflict between traditional and modern. It is right versus wrong. Kanako should never have been in a mental state whereby she would absolve the perpetrator of blame.

Feminism is becoming more and more acceptable in Japan, but the battles are different, and, in truth, it is much harder to break down doors there than anywhere else. Some might say that it is an excuse (Midori's line of thought), and letting the perpetrator go is the problem. But because old school thinking is so entrenched in Japanese society, it's a more convenient place to live at times.

Or that the real issue (notwithstanding the pain some suffer during sexual attacks), is the perpetrator's sense of entitlement over his victim.

In Boulder, the parking lot looks like a car dealership. The black cement and bright yellow paint are orderly if not obtrusive. The disabled parking is painted in pink, which is even more stifling. They stare at each other. Hana is desperate to feel his face.

The CCTV coverage captures their every move. They are famous. But the wigs and makeup and no licence plate help.

They do not go on social media and brag about the eleven dead at the local hotel. Besides, the dead belong to those who have long forgotten their children. And for the dead, the memory of their parents is constantly eviscerated outside Sunset Boulevard strip bars, where their lives sound like an elevator pitch.

There is a mounting pressure for Marco to speak up. He must prove his presence at every turn. Indeed, everyone appears to eat a little more quickly than normal. But as he takes his first bite – a little bit of rice, and then some steamed vegetables – he is not sure what to say anymore.

"Catholicism does not define who I am. In fact, Hana defines me in a lot of ways that far exceed any belief I have found studying religion."

No one speaks.

"I don't defend myself in terms of what Catholicism tells me. I'm always in the driver's seat. In fact, I'm the one understanding in terms of my relationship with Hana, more than anything Catholicism could tell me about our relationship. But Catholics can sometimes give me a little lift, a smile, that can take care of a lot of worries."

Hirato puts some chicken on Marco's plate. The Japanese exchanged between Midori and Hana turns into black noise. Marco pouts, hoping to catch on to at least a little bit of what was just said.

"Hana can study Catholicism with you. She is quite content to go to Rome and be a perfect Catholic girl."

A knock at the back door. Booker Brooks enters the modern house. He is African American and is still awaiting a residency visa. He speaks perfect Japanese and has been living in various parts of Japan for over ten years. He arrived in Tokyo with a Miles Davis cover band, and he decided to stay after falling in love with the country and its people.

Quickly, Hana gets up from her chair and, resembling a trained puppy dog, goes over to Booker and gently pecks him on the cheek. Hirato and Midori don't budge. They motion for Booker to sit down and try the *Hamachi Kama*, or grilled yellowtail collar.

It is Christmas in the middle of summer, when Naomi offers Marco a Sony Walkman and a little stuffed animal. Midori is in a state of panic. She rushes into the kitchen and returns with four very large bottles of beer and places them on the table. She opens each bottle but insists that everyone keep quiet while she tries to listen to their conversation.

Hana scrunches her face and tilts her head to the side and starts to put pressure on Naomi to say more.

It turns out that Kanako believed she had spoken out of turn, and that is what caused the man to turn angry.

Everyone gasps for air at the same time while Naomi communicates the conversation to the table. There is eternal horror among the group.

The ridge of a teacup. The bits of bread on the

65

tablecloth.

The family turns towards Marco.

"God forgives people when sometimes it appears difficult to understand someone. And if he holds God true to his heart."

There are so many references in the Bible that discuss forgiveness. In particular, Mathew 6:14, which says if you forgive those who have sinned against you, the Heavenly Father will forgive you. If it is within our abilities, we must forgive, for that is what the Heavenly Father asks us to do.

Next, Marco quotes Mark 11:25, which describes someone who prays, and to let go of their pain, and forgive, and the Heavenly Father will thus be allowed to forgive their sins. The latter passage resonates with everyone.

"Then God would forgive him for his actions, however grotesque they might appear."

As he mouths the words, he realizes he has made some ground with Hana's family, but then again, no one would be able to tell if he's telling the truth or not.

He rhapsodizes about a great many things: the meaning of God feels weightier here, the feeling of sharing something personal with another person is profound, but soon his broken English puts everyone off. The few clearly expressed Christian words are gone. The bits of Catholic advice have disappeared. The hard, cold English feels like a distant nuisance.

Suddenly, everyone tries to understand Marco through the prism of his Catholic beliefs. But they find that route cumbersome, resulting in awkward, sidelong glances. It turns into a game.

The restaurant is dimly lit. There are black lacquer tables and white floor cushions. There is a drop ceiling at each dining area, with multi-colored lights, emitting a soft, pinky glow. The rules of etiquette are quickly abandoned; it is as though Hana's parents are present with each dish.

The dinner conversation flows easily. There are few missteps during the evening. The décor is easy on the eyes, and the routine of Marco speaking and then Hana quickly translating his thoughts is easily executed. Or else, Hirato will fuss over Marco's empty plate, and order seconds without any discussion.

There are portions of *okonomiyaki* left, or a small dish of *unagi*, eel smothered in tare sauce. Hana asks for a second portion of the miso soup, with thick, green onion.

Hirato, rather unexpectedly, appears to welcome Marco into the family more quickly than the others.

They venture to a nearby bar where they sing Karaoke. Hirato is a big Rod Stewart fan. He claims, "they talk." Marco remains frozen after Hana explains what that means. Suddenly, Hirato turns angrily to Midori and begins to raise his voice.

In a frozen state, Marco has few resources to get an explanation save asking with his eyebrows. And suddenly Hirato turns indignant, but in a quiet sort of way, and so he badgers Midori until they appear to be squabbling unnecessarily about something. The mood changes after several rounds of sake. Hirato orders Japanese whiskey; Midori drinks ochawari, a green tea cocktail.

Marco decides to take the stage. He tests his voice to see how drunk he sounds. He selects "Downtown Train".

Has Hirato just put on his jacket and gone over to the bar? Or has Midori collected all the empty glasses and taken them to the bar?

There is no chance of being dismissive towards Rod Stewart ever again. Of course, Marco was never in the habit of saying anything bad about Rod to begin with. But at the mention of a movie star or music sensation, one always feels welcome to talk about them in a colorful or critical way. A performance moves them, or else something about their personal life. And now Rod is off-limits. When Marco chooses to sing a Willy Nelson classic, the mood changes suddenly. Everyone appears relaxed and carefree. Next, he chooses a Metallica classic, and once more everyone looks upbeat and dances the night away. But there remains some mystery surrounding Rod Stewart.

Hana confesses her father has seen Rod in concert forty times.

"You know how it can get when you really fall for someone."

It is very strange and unusual, but also a crafty bit of hero worship that Marco likes very much. And it is comforting to think Hana and him will always have a connection to Rod Stewart.

Hirato, who is drunk, prances around in his underwear. He clutches an old-fashioned glass, full of Jack Daniels with crushed ice. Marco and Hana sit in the living room and watch *Downton Abbey*.

There is a frantic reach for the door frame, and Hirato avoids falling onto the floor.

Marco and Hana sit up and act polite. And now Marco is transfixed by Hirato's tat work.

Suddenly, Hana turns very still. She is scared. She leans her head against Marco's chest, and suddenly Marco realizes his mistake.

Marco tugs Hana's thick thigh, and she can no longer

deny the connection. There is a side of her that wants to deny her dad's history, but instead she grips Marco's arm to come closer, and her dad disappears into the other room.

"Should we put a shirt on him?"

Hana is blocked from passing through the hallway, as her father lies in the fetal position, purring little snores. The whiskey is displayed as a big, wet mess all over the carpet.

Back in Boulder, the hotel room is a coolish temperature. Marco opens the window. He makes a coffee.

He opens his book bag from uni, takes out a memory chip and attaches it to his MacBook.

He signs into the VPN. He inserts the chip and downloads the data. He snaps the chip into two. He runs to the other end of the underground parking lot and uses his knee to bend the laptop in half. He is acting bizarre, smashing the laptop on the ground.

Hana is alone in her parents house. She turns white and smiles for the first time. She likes the challenge of being away from each other. Marco promises her they will make a home back in Rome. He will find a job. And they will begin the tasks of becoming responsible, entertaining, and trying to understand the human condition. Hana is a little embarrassed by her tears now; all she can see is happiness in their life.

The plane breaks through the clouds, and everyone sounds a little panicky. Marco rests his eyes on the wing, at all the little bits of metal that vibrate as the plane rises higher and higher and displays more and more power.

Suddenly, the turbulence stops. They are on a bed of clouds. The seat belt sign is turned off. A man stands up and goes into the overhead compartment and removes his laptop. A woman in a thick sweater follows her baby who crawls up the aisle. And Marco continues to glare out the window at the silver wing. The little TV screen in front of him says "-60 degrees Celsius".

Ecclesiastes 11:4: "He who watches the wind will not sow and he who looks at the clouds will not reap."

He taps the screen in front of him, and scrolls through the movies. He is indignant about the Heavenly Father's mystery, and the clouds are the last thing he wants to see. His eyelids are heavy, but he remains awake.

And God, he thinks, is not beautiful. Nor the creator of love, for quite obviously love is far too powerful a force to accept in our lives. And the magnificence of the clouds pervades him. And now he breathes heavily. And he admits his faith in God has nothing to do with love. He repeats these words to himself over and over. And then he signs up for Twitter.

Italy

Marco's room faces a busy street. The sounds of traffic fill the room. He can hear the neighbors getting into their cars and going to work. He wants to be part of a group that goes to work each day.

The breakfast table is bare, save for a single daisy in a green, Italian wine bottle. Serena enters the kitchen and goes over to the fridge, where she pours herself a tall glass of red wine. Marco recognizes his mother's patterns. The functioning alcoholic. They never discuss it. The alcoholism just plays into their lives. There will be weeks when Serena won't touch the stuff. And then suddenly, it is a tall glass of red wine for breakfast, and life and death will play out until she can't take the booze anymore. It usually lasts about four days...until fear takes over. Marco figures she is on day three of a rather serious one. It might end at any moment. It also depends on who she is seeing.

She lights a cigarette, and then balances the cigarette box on the table. She looks at Marco and smiles. They are best friends. But each also hates something about the other. For example, Marco hates that his mother sleeps with men who she meets at the neighborhood bar. She drinks. Her life erupts into melodrama. And Serena hates Marco's independence. He tends to disappear to another country and make connections with new people and start a life.

But the differences also highlight how much is

irreconcilable about their relationship. More often than not they end up steering their conversations into the wrong lanes, and then grudgingly try and find some peaceful way of going about their own lives as safely and peacefully as possible.

Inside the tiny kitchen, with the worn, walnut table and chipped, white, wooden chairs, it feels like a safe destination more than all of Expedia's vacation packages combined.

For her part, she feels his life should remain inside the apartment, listening to the sounds from the street below, and meeting in the kitchen, and fussing about who is going to cook breakfast.

Serena reaches over and grabs the bottle of wine; however, a vase accidently falls over and smashes on the tiled floor.

As a young boy, Marco was directed to enter the game. His coach approached him on the sidelines and said a few words. He looked over at his mother, who stood beside Aldo (her brother, Marco's uncle), and they appeared more nervous than excited to be at the game. Marco took a nice pass on the right side and then cut through the middle and then past the centre line before pushing the ball up the field. Marco motioned to put the ball through, which he took by heading the ball to a bounce on his right side and then shot one past the goalkeeper into the top right corner. The coach ran onto the field in the opposite direction before finding his players and they all cheered uproariously.

Serena screams as the vase shatters on the floor. He juggles the football. He counts out loud: forty-two, forty-three. Diego comes out of his apartment. Marco sneaks a look at him, and Diego knows immediately his role; Diego: Fifty, fifty-one…

In Boulder, the conference room is partitioned off from another conference room, similar in size (about two hundred square feet).

You enter a regular sized door, and there is a meeting table set up like in *The Godfather.* Hana sees the counters. She plunks down the duffle bag of money. Next, a logistics table, with white, linen tablecloths (the ones that could be cut up and used as heavy napkins), and heavy silver trays, replete with scrambled eggs, crepes with jam, Canadian sausage, and toast. A tray of OJ already poured, and two cappuccino machines.

Sweat pours off his forehead, or a tap and glide action against the conference room door. He even puts his toe against the door to ensure that it is shut. Next, he looks at Hana. He pulls out a handgun.

"Go to the park!"
But Marco ignores his mother and continues to juggle the ball.

The door slams. As Marco walks towards the kitchen, he can hear Diego in the stairwell, explaining he is borrowing the soccer ball.

Marco looks at the shattered glass in the garbage bin.
"I bought you that vase for Christmas."
"I never liked it."
"It was a present."
"Buy me better presents."

Later, they head out for dinner. The airy restaurant is famous for its Northern Italian cuisine, which includes pizza *al taglio*, *saltimbocca*, which is veal cutlets wrapped in prosciutto, and sage, Jewish fried artichokes, and the famous porchetta, which is cooked with liver, garlic, and fresh fennel. It includes a terrace, and a thick, lime-green, pinstriped awning. The tables and chairs are a vibrant red.

The restaurant has a dark, brick interior, with a wide hallway at the very back which leads to the washroom and the kitchen. There is a little fountain in the middle, which has a fancy LED light which makes the water glow. Kids like to stand around the fountain and throw centesimos into the shallow water and make a wish.

The walls are covered in reproductions of Botticelli and DaVinci. Oli, who waits tables, is an unwelcoming host. He seats guests at any table he prefers, and then argues with them until they accept his choice. He never speaks to the cook, which, curiously, creates an odd experience inside the restaurant, for the open kitchen allows everyone to witness the kitchen dynamic.

Caves are easily lit. Mountain tops are the fury of an open prairie. If your execution is performed well, your reputation will grow in all reaches of the world. And we'll try and get a film made based on your life story. Public eliminations are the pièce de résistance.

Fame is not welcome news to Oli. The *Roma Times* gives the restaurant four out of five stars. The only reason he lost a star was because the host was "born nasty."

But four out of five stars is still too high. Besides, Oli does not need the pressure of a famous kitchen, for the moment the chef leaves, their reputation is going to suffer immensely.

Giorgio stands in the entranceway. Serena likes his wet, greasy hair. Or his motorcycle tees, the sleeves of which he rolls up on both arms. He wears jeans and red, leather boots. He has a cigarette in his mouth. He prefers a close shave but is too busy in the mornings doing "shit". And, besides, he enjoys the reaction of shaving at his desk with an electrical shaver. He works at a call centre part-time.

"Can I smoke?"

"What do you think?"

"Do you have a terrace?"

Both his parents smoke. Giorgio believes it is his moral duty to at least voice these words, as though he is one of the last ones holding out for a different set of laws from those prescribed by the government. People are a little intimidated by his presence. And he makes few manoeuvres to lessen the attention.

Boot stomps, but not oppressive, turn into a slight tune, as Serena holds her palm on the back of Giorgio's neck and kisses him. She starts to pull him towards the terrace. Giorgio greets everyone with a polite handshake, and then pours himself a glass of red wine. He places the bottle of red back down on the table, which is surrounded by plates of arancini, antipasto bites, focaccia bread, and even pasta chips. He holds his glass of wine high above his receding hairline, the thick wine glass shimmers under the sparkles of a freshly stuccoed ceiling. The group chuckles as they toast a Wednesday night gathering.

Marco gets a FaceTime message from Hana.

"I miss you more than I can say."

"I miss you!"

One of the great joys of the job is the chance to play God. Suddenly, you are in a domestic life, and you have the chance to contemplate the past, present, and future. But it is the job where you find God's meaning.

Serena likes Giorgio's argumentative nature.

And Serena likes the friendly faces, for she knows that people like Giorgio will come and go, and her friends understand her likes and dislikes. And no one is judging her. The same script plays itself over and over. Serena feels safe.

They break up after neither one remembers being with the other person the night before. And they cringe at the rumours. What's more, they regard the lack of memory as more interesting than being with the other person.

Marco flops down and tries to fall asleep. Serena marches into Marco's room and screams that her son is unlovable.

"So, he can claim he's my father? Or later ask you for a loan so he can resume a construction company? No, mother!"

Marco focusses on the birds singing. He rolls his eyes and now he recalls Giorgio entering his room in the middle of the night, asking for money.

"Why can't you just get drunk and come home and pass out on a bed like everyone else?"

"Your father would have hated you."

"Yeah, it looks like Giorgio needs some help."

He puts on a sweatshirt. He is distracted by the running water.

The kitchen table includes Natto, grilled fish, ohitashi, and pickles. And a glass of freshly squeezed OJ. Hana comes running from around the corner.

They scream with excitement. And then a series of hugs and kisses. Hana cannot stop herself from jumping up and down. And Marco laughs in accompaniment. Even Serena claps in rhythm.

Everyone sits down and eats a traditional Japanese breakfast, which includes *tamagoyaki*, nori, some tofu and veg. Hana arrives in the middle of the night. Serena is sworn to secrecy not to tell Marco her plans. Hana calls from Frankfurt to confirm the address, and she ends up speaking to Giorgio.

"I didn't buy a return ticket."

"What did customs say?"

"I told them I was meeting my Italian husband, and then he turned quiet."

The domestic life and the job are two separate worlds. The job is a much more important commitment...because (drum roll) we don't have laws. In that sense, we are a much freer society. Individual rights are not important, because we don't have a list of things you can and cannot do.

Hana sleeps for fifteen hours. Marco tries to explain their plans. Serena doesn't seem at all interested. Instead, she continues to drink and later meets Giorgio at a local restaurant.

"Do you finally get that I am getting married?"

"Not if she doesn't wake up."

"She has jet lag."

"She better get a job, because I'm not paying for her groceries."

They lie on the bed. Rome is much more interesting

than London, Paris, or Madrid. The Vatican is just a stone's throw away, where some of the world's finest minds are dedicated to questions of Christianity. Hana remains indifferent. She snuggles close to Marco, and they reminisce about Boulder. She recalls the time she threw the celery stick across the dance floor.

They attend an outdoor screening of *The Searchers*, and the famous ending where John Wayne stands in the doorway - the barren, desolate prairie in the background. This turns into a humorous side act for Marco, who imitates John Wayne whenever he finds a doorway.

They decide to go for a walk. They stop at a grocer's. A rolling entrance store front. The freezer gives off a loud, humming noise.

The counter is replete with homemade pastries, Tiramisu, *Pasticciotto leccese*, and a tray of pizza with red sauce. Nico, the owner, reaches over and offers Hana his hand.

"Italian, and nothing else."

"Oh."

"Yeah, he's a true Italian guy. Very proud."

The Book does not always have its way with its criminal past. In other words, there are some criminals who did it the right way and others who did it the wrong way. Some might think that sounds like an oxymoron, but even in the criminal world there are rules. And the rules cannot be broken. There is one gangster, however, who stands out as someone who followed the rules, and for that reason we honour his name: Albert Anastasia.

A formidable gangster, he would one day be in charge of the five families of the Cosa Nostra. Some of his contemporaries include The Gambino family, Vito Genovese, Joe Adonis, Lucky Luciano, Frank Costello, and Benjamin "Bugsy" Siegel.

During the prohibition era, Anastasia earned a reputation as the hired hitman for Lucky Luciano.

The 1930s was a transformative time for mobsters. The Lower East Side created more millionaires than Wall Street.

Anastasia had three tough cases against him in the years 1928, '32, and '33 respectively. Prosecutors were bragging they finally had the piece of the puzzle to put him away for good.

And then Anastasia made his move: he undressed the prosecution's case one piece at a time. Next, all the critical eyewitnesses disappeared. The prosecution woke up one morning and realized they didn't have a case anymore; they didn't have a bus ticket to get to city hall.

The post-war years in New York City were pretty exciting, but they were also very risky. The New York five families had a lot of disputes with each other. And it turned out the Gambino family were interested in making a move. It was only a matter of time, and then, one day, while he was getting a shave at the barber's, Anastasia was gunned down and killed.

What you must understand is that the US government would hire him to protect the New York stock yards from Nazi infiltration. Despite a checkered past, he was honoured as a hero by his country.

La Fortuna is an affordable, family-owned restaurant near Marco's apartment.

La Fortuna is a second home for Marco, as he has a close relationship with Riccardo, his former football coach. Riccardo's parents, Paula and Marti, run La Fortuna. Paula assumes control of the kitchen and Marti oversees the dining room. The roles switched only after Marti had a heart attack. He used to arrive at the restaurant early each morning, check the deliveries, and oversea the two-cook kitchen. A bottle of red by 10 am and two packs of Camels before he strolls back to his home a few blocks away. The turnaround is nothing short of a miracle. The floating bar has been replaced with a rock garden. He merely greets customers these days. Paula brings him a staff meal each night which consists of grilled veg and a filet of fish.

Riccardo is part owner and works four nights a week. He is a celebrity in his own rite: he made the under eighteens Italian team. And later, the under twenties. He coached soccer for a long time. He met a young Marco, and eventually helped him climb the prodigious ladder. First, as a daring mid-fielder and, later, as a scolding threat in the right center forward position. Riccardo believed Marco had all the skills to eventually wear an Italian jersey.

Neither one has achieved any success on the football pitch. Riccardo began to gamble excessively which eventually killed his football career. And Marco, upon making the under sixteens team, was told by doctors that he had an irregular heartbeat and was forbidden to touch the ball again.

Eventually, Riccardo was let go by his local club, and he has begun repaying his debts. Indeed, the mob pressure became so animated and colorful – letters written in blood, or fish heads in the crisper (once in the toilet bowl) – that he began to repay his debts in earnest.

And then, one lazy spring morning, Riccardo was

informed his debts had been wiped clean. The word on the street is that the boss of the cartel has died and his papers are in a bad mess, but his replacement likes footballers.

When you are in the middle of domestic life you have the advantage of looking back on the past, enjoying the present, and anticipating the future. However, there is no time continuum when it comes to the job. You might be asked to lend a hand, and you are expected to say "yes", right off the hop.
However, time stops when you take on a job. The player's location and time have no meaning when they are on the job. Just get it done.

Serena believes Marco stands a chance of making it on his own. Or soccer is somehow an easy escape from the real-life pitfalls of life. And because of her strengths and tutelage, and making Marco always feel better, he settles in his life and embraces academics.

Hana can see Marco and Riccardo share a strong bond. But she also sees their disappointments. She does not know whether to encourage Marco to find out the meaning of their friendship, or else turn diminutive and act passive. And she does not deny that she must frequently wear a mask that suits some stranger and, being Japanese, this act is repeated all too frequently. She weighs her options and decides to lower her head and pretend not to understand what is going on.

Marti places a ceramic bowl in front of Hana, and then one in front of Marco. She puts her mouth to the spoon. The *Ribollita*, a bread and bean porridge, takes her to another place.

The waiter returns with a baguette and a dish of curled butter.

Marco recommends Hana should try the pasta.

"Why didn't we get to order?" Hana inspects the other tables.

"This is the *Plat du jour*. But just for us."

"Oh."

"I trust them. They are rarely wrong about what I like."

"But how do they know what I like?"

"Oh, Italians are like that."

Riccardo discards soccer at every turn. And ever since he quit drugs, he realizes all of his memories of football are clouded by his past drug use. Some things are just too difficult to discard. Marco used to meet a counsellor and discuss his early exit. Marco must find another hobby and forget about football. And besides "you have a chance to be part of a much larger community: football was not meant to be."

Marco might have played football, but he is much more interesting as a human being. But Riccardo's predicament is different, for he was truly great at playing football. And today, he resembles someone always trying to find their way back to the pitch.

Marco has no intention of entering any narrative when it comes to Giorgio. His mom must stand up for herself. If one can't stand up against the likes of Giorgio, what hope is there for any of us?

The communication is very clear and unambiguous: she is going away for a few days; if Giorgio calls, tell him she has died.

"How does your mother know that it is not serious?"

"Because there was no screaming probably."

Diego juggles the soccer ball. And reports that Serena has gone away for a few days.

"Give me the ball back."

"Your mom said I could play with it until she got back."

"It belongs to me."

"Come on, Marco, don't be mean just because you have a real friend."

"That doesn't make sense. And if you lose that ball, you're on the hook."

There is the constant need to go out in Rome.

At a certain point, you find it hard to balance the domestic life with the job. But that is the task of the layering process. Indeed, that is when the job will suddenly reveal its true meaning. And stories and anecdotes and bills to pay. Meanwhile, we'll be setting you up for your next job.

They make supper: Spaghetti Carbonaro. Instinctively, Hana wants to put Soya sauce on the table. The same is true whenever Hana cooks. The recipe eventually wins. They make concessions in order to keep the recipes as original as possible. Neither one is willing to close the door on their own culture. They re-work their favorite recipes and include the other persons tastes. And soon they are chuffed with the fusion cuisine.

Their union will only be secure once they have established an economic union. Hana is eager to work, but upon speaking to the Japanese consulate, such an idea is impossible until they marry.

A domestic person's poverty is like an athlete who attends training camp overweight. In other words, keep your house in check.

Marco takes Hana to his favorite frozen yogurt shop. They stand in front of the foggy curved glass which covers the most sought-after frozen yogurts in Rome. Hana gazes at the cardboard cut-outs of mango, banana, and passionfruit that dangle from the ceiling. The top selections include cotton candy, cookies & cream, and California cake. The counterperson takes a modest scoop of chocolate, and then some peppermint. The employee's smile is unforgettable, and she helps another client before she'll take a compliment.

Eventually, the great media empires of the world, like the *New York Times, The Guardian*, and the *Washington Post* will disappear after a social media revolution. They will fade away because there are far too many competing factors in the world to control their internal filtering systems. They have begun to censor people, and their choice to censor is being applied sporadically.

"Could you imagine being the one who has to send Donald Trump an email and say he is cut off from Twitter?"

"Yeah."

"I mean, that is not what the system is designed to do. And to me that is the essential bug of the entire system."

"Yeah."

Information is shared in such a way that it purports to be the only information available on the subject. No other source can exist. Trump is a perfect example of someone who does not understand the breadth of social media. He is always talking to "his people". He is always trying to build his empire. The Twitter ethos can tell immediately that Trump is not helping their commitment towards a social universe. Look at Russian hackers who supported Trump, and who used social media to spread fake news. They do not actually support any one person, but instead try and steer an ideology of false information. False information is not about singling someone out as better than another person, it merely acts to clog the system with false information.

In other words, spreading false information is a problem about false information. Indirectly, someone like Trump, the Great Apricot Croissant in the sky, might be crowned the winner. But the reason for his title has nothing to do with him per se, but rather the lack of checks and balances which give him a sense of entitlement.

The phone rings. Neither one likes their life. They hate the caller. And they mock the timing. They remain quiet until all the cheering and absurdity about answering the phone clears.

The weight of the Boulder crew. They dare not mention their names. They search for the silence which they've enjoyed these past few weeks. They fling their costumes across the floor, and they know their next move.

Aldo, Marco's uncle, calls to complain that Serena has arrived at his home drunk. Marco drives at breakneck speeds. Hana looks out the window. His silence is intolerable. He is consumed by his mother's life. And it is her bad habits that cause all his worries.

He looks at her black hair, her ivory skin, and inky

eyes. And she turns and glares at Marco, who is not expecting her to look at him. He glares at the red light.

At the side of the house is a one-hundred-foot knock-off Louis Vuitton water hose, set to a timer. Aldo sinks deeper into the well-kept lawn, a few yards from Hana, when suddenly the hose erupts, and Marco becomes the lead in a slapstick comedy.

Aldo is the owner of three car dealerships in Rome and two others in Spain. Aldo was very poor for most of his life. And then he met Tina, and soon she was pregnant. And then suddenly Aldo decided that he could no longer be that person with a baby on the way. He continued non-stop for several years until he earned enough to buy a used dealership. He ventured into other countries and repeated the process. Now, children play soccer with his dealership name emblazed on their jerseys. He sponsors a beauty contest in twenty cities in Italy.

Aldo has made every sacrifice possible to control his sister's life, and he remains steadfast about his kingdom, and easily ignores the concerns of others.

He was once a little boy, and Aldo gave Marco his first kit and a soccer ball. He is the most perfect nephew in the world. He has become his sister's representative, who comes up with nonsensical arguments to stay out of the family business, which Aldo thinks he can easily dismantle.

The gates open. The three-storey house is a mix of architectural styles. Tina is in charge of the interior design. One room might be baroque with portraiture, while another room is minimalist and sculptured. The chihuahua discovers he can enter any room and trigger the stereo to blast because of the light sensors at the floor board entrance. Aldo admits the house is slightly over-engineered.

Aldo continues to water the lawn and scolds his two children.

"Can you hear her shrieking?" Aldo searches the backyard.

"Are you sure that's my mom?"

"Do you think my wife would shriek like that?"

Sebastian, the cook, stands on the pool deck and looks over the garden. He returns a few moments later with a bowl of ice cream for Serena. She takes the ice cream and throws it against the fountain. It is a perfect segway for Aldo to come over and begin a shouting match all over again.

Aldo continues to antagonize his sister. Some things will never change. But Marco will not have it. He brings her a margarita with a pink umbrella and puts it on the side table. Marco asks that they pray. He is merely asking that they find some peace before it is too late.

Hana stands in the middle of the unkempt Japanese garden. Her father calls her on the iPhone which brings the hardness of the situation even closer to her.

The children run from room to room. And Hana can see Peter Pan plotting a night of adventures. Her father repeats that he is on his way to Rome.

"I am coming to Rome to see you."

"But I have no home to share with you."

"Find out if I am allowed to see my daughter?"

Hana drops the iPhone.

Aldo's presence puts pressure in all the wrong places. The night feels lighter than before, the alcohol and drugs have had their time, and, of course, it is something to four in the morning. The night's events, truth be told, are merely the commonplace rifts of a deranged man. In the end, there is some peace, as Serena is a little further away from the violence.

Marco goes over to the flowerbed, falls to his knees, and begins to throw punches at the ground. His face is blurry with tears. His chest pounds. Serena comes over, and they hug. Eventually they laugh.

In a garbled voice, Marco harangues his mother. Because they are so close, it sounds insincere (not at all nasty), and they haven't really accomplished anything in their meeting.

Aldo lights a joint and continues to stare blankly at his sister. He repeats that he throws Giorgio from the property when he finds him trying to climb over the fence searching for Serena. He ends up spending the afternoon insulting his sister for acknowledging a person like Giorgio. Next, he harangues Marco for allowing Giorgio to stay at the apartment "which I own!"

As they drive home, a car tries to pass, blinding Marco in the rear-view mirror and the side mirrors. Marco clutches the rear-view mirror.

The evening transitions into the early morning hours. Serena sits on the leather couch at Aldo's and watches TV. Or else she stumbles into the kitchen. She falls on the floor. But Aldo has a craving for fried eggs. He gently walks around his sister and begins to cook. As he drunkenly plates the eggs, he growls that she'd better be gone before the kids get up in the morning.

"Their father is full of cancer!"

The life of a criminal requires him to keep everyone with whom he has contact in the dark. It is layers of silence, smothered in paranoia, surrounded by more untruths. An occasional glimmer of normalcy will appear only when the criminal life feels too stifling.

Another time, Aldo was arrested for misdemeanor battery. Aldo continues to deny the events, saying he might have pushed Marco during an altercation, but he never once thru the kitchen table at his sister.

There are countless layers of camouflage surrounding the career criminal. And the innocent glimpses of another life are few and far between. But ultimately the criminal lifestyle rejects any other kind of life. Any respite is always thought of as suspicious.

There have been lots of situations where domestics have tried to escape the unit. That is why it is important to silently and creatively respect your role. You might end up being silent for a long time, but your silence is actually a great bounty, a test, for a once in a lifetime reckoning. In the appendix, under "Heist", you will see references to jobs in Massachusetts during the 1930s and 1940s. You may want to read the Heist section more than once.

Marco strides over the hardwood floors and pecks Hana on the lips and then on the neck. She insists that Marco should quickly get dressed.

"My father is very protective."

"I think he would be a very good influence on my mother."

"He is just very traditional Japanese."

89

Marco tidies the counter. He peers outside and sees a group of men gathered at the corner. They don't look familiar. One of the men, who has a round face with stubble and a marine brush cut, catches Marco staring at them. They appear disinterested, and huddle on the street, in vendor tuque or an Adidas track suit. Some of them smoke, and one wears a three-piece suit.

If one succumbs to the games of intimidation found in Rome, one may never end up leaving one's apartment. A gust of fresh air is accompanied by a hood in a black, woolen mask, sometimes wielding a knife. And besides, Marco recognizes the culprit. He turns on the cold water, and now he sees the disgust of his choices. And he sees the dedication of these men on the street. Of choosing to live by the sword. And not care about the repercussions. He taps the side of the sink. And now he searches further for something ironic, sad, melancholic – anything to dispel the realization that he is part of their world.

Hana remains aloof about her job prospects. She has saved enough money to help with the costs. She occasionally pays for a meal out. She is hopeful she will find a job in social media or something like that once they get settled.

The position involves taking pictures of campus life and covering university events and posting them on social media.

During supper, which includes *Cacio e Pepe*, and regarding which Hana has trouble figuring out how pepper and cheese can taste so good, Marco tells his mother that his lack of job offers is because he looks too Italian. Marco adds that Joe, his uncle, who has fair skin and blue eyes, would have felt slighted by all their talk.

Serena adds he needs to be more chilled about his look, and besides Joe ate too much alfredo pasta which made him have blond hair and blue eyes.

"Mamamia!"

Marco looks around at all the impressive buildings inside the Vatican. And he is suddenly caught up in a group of touristy fascinations.

Four cardinals walk slowly up the street. They each wear a scarlet uniform, a mozetta or small cape, and a biretta or square cap with four ridges. Each wears a unique cross around their neck. Marco goes towards the entrance.

"Marco!"

Occasionally he used to help at weddings, funerals, and christenings.

There is an unyielding number of memories and introspection that follows, but little to do with religion, as he feels as though he has debated these ideas constantly since his youth. And strangely, he pitches his memories into an altogether different destination. A dog he used to own, the time he took a corner kick, enjoying a meal with his family.

The relationship has never been stronger. Indeed, Marco races to reconnect with the Church. He tries to reconcile his relationship with Hana. Or else, he wants to discuss family and hear the cardinals' opinions. Cardinal Peter continues to hold his arm to prevent him from falling over (perhaps he recognizes that the quest into religious ideas is soon tempered with the realities of the here and now). And Marco is on the job hunt. He needs to get his life back in order. Marco feels the arm of the cardinal and tries to create some nostalgia between the two men. Does such a thing exist? And now Cardinal Peter looks deep into Marco's eyes, and they have a poetic meeting of minds.

Serena has always been very protective of Marco, and she is very suspicious of the Church, for it is well known that young boys are often preyed upon. Serena once confronted Cardinal Peter about his obsession with Marco.

There is some shuffling and a little scramble from the cardinals, for they notice that Cardinal Peter has taken an interest in the young man. Cardinal Peter smiles at his friends, takes a fast drag of his cig, and motions that he will be a minute or so.

Soon, Marco was building a prodigious report card: outside football practice, he attended mass several times a week, twice on Sundays. Holidays and special holidays are booked at the church. And he absorbed all their stories, staying up late with his mom.

"No," Cardinal Peter answered Serena. "We will make sure that Marco finds the straight and narrow, which you've managed to sabotage up until now."

The two men laugh at how futile that appears to have worked. Cardinal Peter smiles and says he will pray for Serena later today. He feels blessed to have seen Marco again. The close friends walk around the empty streets and Cardinal Peter listens attentively to Marco's past pursuits. He is particularly interested in hearing about Hana. He likes the sound of Hana's father, who pushes Marco to think about Italy's role during World War II. Cardinal Peter says he will pray for Hirato.

"But I am no longer religious as I once was."

"His Holiness just needs someone to upload his picture, and some text, and send it around the world."

"Really?"

"Yeah, we need to boost his numbers on his Twitter account."

A group of police officers mingle on the street. A young executive in high heels walks awkwardly towards the front doors of the *Palazzo del Governatorato*, the main administrative offices in the Vatican. A group of nuns hand out white plastic bags of food to the poor. Cardinal Peter twiddles his thumbs like he is writing a message.

"I will have to think about this for a little while."

If Marco replies something different, say, "yes, I am interested", the cardinal might dismiss the offer immediately, and say he shouldn't have said anything. By postponing his answer, it works to safeguard their friendship. And both men are keenly aware of the sinister contract they have made. Marco wants to speak to his mom and Hana, and make sure working for God's representative is proper. At the very least, he will be expected to dust off some of his Catholic beliefs, and make sure he looks the part. His Holiness, Cardinal Peter explains, expects to meet someone who believes in God and manages their life accordingly.

Marco is embarking on a career path not unlike landing a good job at IBM, Apple, or Coca-Cola. But His Holiness is even more important than all of those companies. Serena has yet to weigh in on the announcement. She reminds Marco about the time she met Cardinal Peter and how he treated her.

"They are offering you a job because Cardinal Peter treated me like shit that one time when you were just a little bambino!"

Marco brainstorms the problem. On the one hand, his mom is acting overprotective. But, on the other hand, her words are confrontational, when, in truth, there are a few decent people still working at the Vatican.

Her worries are misplaced, and Cardinal Peter is a perfect cardinal. Someone who always looks out for Marco's best interests. Indeed, Cardinal Peter has always been a gentleman and only wants Marco to survive.

Serena goes over to Hana and holds her shoulders. She tries to speak English, which sounds like a very innocent Italian woman without any desire to learn another language.

"I'm just trying to protect my baby. And Cardinal Peter was mean. He's always treated me badly."

"Why?"

"Because he knows I am right to protect my bambino as much as I do."

Marco takes his mom in his arms and begins to twirl around the room. Hana turns up the music.

Marco and Hana hold hands. The job offer becomes bigger than what it's worth. But the pressure rolls forward.

Hana reflects she has never felt further from home than right now. And suddenly, she reflects upon her experience in Rome, finding herself in another boring conversation (the weather, the mail has not arrived, the milk tastes sour, or we've stopped at a railway crossing), when suddenly someone uses an original turn of phrase, and once more they race to make their union perfect.

Back in Boulder, Marco's feet are stuck under a thick arm. And Hana has a glow about her. The duffle bags of money are neatly stacked by the door. He wrestles to get his leg free. There is a faint hint of smoke that rises over the pile of dead bodies.

He stumbles towards the door, turns to Hana for a moment, then robotically takes the silencer and taps a few rounds into a couple of heavies from the Delaware crew.

He thinks about his relationship with God.

As he looks at his mother, he can tell she is thinking the same thing. She turns the entire experience on Marco. Marco holds his mother's hand. Serena nudges for another glass of wine.

Giorgio pays someone in the neighborhood to watch Serena. He shows up at the party that Aldo has organized to celebrate Marco's new job. Giorgio approaches Serena and touches her shoulder. Aldo gets up from his seat and escorts Giorgio into the back alley. Next, the paramedics spend an inordinate amount of time using tweezers to remove cigarette butts from Giorgio's inner ear.

The party continues late into the night.

Aldo stands up and raises his glass. He clears his throat before he begins to speak.

"I want to congratulate Marco for assuming his rightful duty in working as the messenger of God."

"I'm not choosing what His Holiness decides to say."

"Sure, you are." Aldo looks a little shocked at Marco's lack of manners.

"No, I'm just posting stuff for him online."

"You're part of the process of what His Holiness hears from God, and then you put it up."

"Yeah, I guess so."

"That's important. Your grandmother would be proud

of you. God bless her soul. And make sure you translate what I just said to your girl! Once you're ready, Marco, you can always come and work for me!"

"Yeah, we'll see what happens." Marco appears ready to leave, given no one understands his role at the Vatican.

"Just work for God for a while and keep your beak clean. And don't embarrass your family."

Aldo senses that Marco is no longer paying attention, and so Aldo seeks Serena's attention.

"Right, Serena?"

"Shut up."

"I nearly killed a man for you tonight. And that's what I get?"

"You just told my son he should work for you after he works for His Holiness."

"I need somebody to help me with the business."

"Just leave him alone. And be happy he works for a legitimate organization."

"You're telling me His Holiness is legit?"

Marco smashes his glass of wine down on the table.

"Would you both please stop!"

The back alley is lit by a single streetlight. A heavy-set crow causes some wires to swing, casting a glossy shadow on the street below. There is enough light to trigger a few light gulps of wine from Giorgio who sits on a discarded metal chair at the side of the alley. He smokes and talks on his cell phone. Marco and Hana walk gingerly past. And suddenly, Marco feels obliged to explain what really happened tonight. Hana is uncomfortable with the violence. It is how things are done in the neighborhood. Hana grips Marco's arm as though she understands. They continue up the street – it begins to make sense. Indeed, a little while after, it feels innocent and normal. Marco stops. He gently manoeuvres Hana against the lamp post. He moves his hand down her back, and she holds one of his arms. She places her cold hand against his naval – Marco smiles and grabs her wrist. They continue down the street. They laugh and stumble back to the apartment.

Cardinal Peter enters the room. He offers a welcoming smile before he speaks.

"I see you cleared security."

"Yes, it only took two days."

"Well, the big man in the sky needs to make sure everything is going right."

"I hope I got paid for that interrogation." Marco immediately regrets the words he has spoken.

"Yes. I've informed His Holiness about you."

"Oh?"

"He's looking forward to meeting you."

"Yes, of course. I hope I'll be able to carry the conversation as well as the American Ambassador."

"Oh, never mind. Come on, let's go and make introductions. He's just finished prayers. And then he'll be off on a trip to Africa."

The walls are covered in art. The orange uniforms of the Swiss Guard are loud and godly. They walk briskly down the long corridor. Cardinal Peter discusses official business. And they already feel like they've accomplished a lot.

They enter a large room, where the Swiss Guard stand at the entrance. The walls are covered in 16th century frescoes.

Cardinal Peter approaches His Holiness and introduces

Marco.

"This is the new social media expert I mentioned."

"Oh, perfect, the one who will make me famous?"

"Yes." Cardinal Peter smiles and looks at Marco to make sure he is OK to speak.

Marco immediately forgets the proper protocol for addressing His Holiness. He decides to wing it anyway.

"It is my great pleasure to make your acquaintance, my Great Holiness."

"God bless you, my son. It is Marco?"

"Yes."

"I would ask that you try and be as kind as possible when you use my image or quote me."

"Of course, Holy Father."

"I need as much help as I can get. I pray, but I need people to *see* that I am praying. I think that will help people who need healing."

"Of course, Holy Father."

"In other words, I'm not asking you to take my picture. I need you to communicate the fact that I care for people. We want to move their souls."

As His Holiness takes a few steps forward – the contrast of his white cassock against medieval tables, modern flat screen, ancient ideas – a skimpy-looking bird with bulgy eyes lands on the ledge. There is an undeniable collision of nature, sounds, and feelings inside the room. Marco is transfixed by the red papal shoes and the pectoral cross.

In Boulder, Marco returns to the hotel room. The white, twisty hallway carpet. He hangs up his jacket and puts his shoes by the door. He places the clown mask on the pillow. He grabs the mickey of Johnnie Walker from the bedside table – with the heavy lamp and the sticky clicker – and takes a small sip. He pours the rest of the whisky down the toilet.

Here lie eleven dead bodies. He repeats the line "here lie eleven dead bodies!" over and over again, like he is an important poet at an important reading. He is tired of reciting his poem, and is now overcome with anger, as he learns a band from Minnesota has decided to use his line for their next single.

He can see a group of cardinals leaving the building. One of the Cardinals stops and lights a cigarette and looks up at the window.

Most of the pictures are sent to the bin. The ones he intends to keep, he will send a reply (which includes a liability clause) and thank the person for sending a picture to His Holiness.

"Remember, he is just a human being like you and me."

"Of course."

"And decide if you are going to call him your Great Holiness, or something else. But don't use both names."

"Yes, I was going to ask you that…?"

"I don't think he noticed."

"Right."

"OK, so maybe we'll get started with his Twitter account. We need to build that traffic I was telling you about."

"I was looking at some pictures."

"Good. Nice job today. Your mother would be proud."

"Thank you."

He enters a corner store and buys a soft pack of Camel Lights, a Snickers bar, and can of Heineken. He turns down a back alley, opens the beer, and smokes a cigarette. On paper he must increase His Holiness's twitter account. Cardinal Peter insists they must reach one million followers. He mentions several names like Pelé, Messi, and Neymar Jr., who all have over one million followers.

"His Holiness has nothing in common with football."

"How so?"

Cardinal Peter is in no mood to partake in the conversation. He moans about the former soccer great Maradona, who recently passed away because of sloppy medical advice. He is the famous footballer who once scored a famous goal against England to win the 1986 World Cup. That was the game where Maradona used "the hand of God" to put the ball in the back of the net. The Cardinal insists Maradona is famous because he was Catholic.

Each step is a major obstacle, and as he climbs (he is disgusted by the chipped walls, and dusty, cement stairs), he moans at the prospect of going home.

"Besides, His Holiness knows the Bible inside out, he could easily counter the "the hand of God" goal, with countless razzle dazzle tricks of his own."

Diego sits on the floor and looks bored. Marco offers a tired smile but is more focussed on the chatter on the other side of the thin door. His mother's laughter puts a smile on everyone's face.

"Why don't you go outside and play soccer?"

"I don't have a ball."

"Since when?" Marco raises his hands in disbelief.

"The Chinese woman?!"

"Are you talking about Hana? She's Japanese."

"What's the difference, Marco?"

"A meatball is not chicken parmesan."

"She doesn't speak Italian, Marco?"

"Just barge in and find the ball and take it. Don't worry about it."

Marco turns on the radio and sits down to eat. Next, he grabs the soccer ball and tosses it into the hallway. He can hear Diego scampering down the stairs, thanking Marco for the ball.

Marco removes a bottle of red wine from his briefcase. Hana cannot stop giggling. She looks at Marco, who is busy eating his pasta. He senses the burden of their impatience, but the rehearsal in his mind is unfinished. He is undecided where to begin.

Serena looks around the table and notices an uncomfortable silence. Immediately, she takes a sip of wine.

"Must we act polite in order to hear about your day?"

"No, it was fine."

"Did you meet His Holiness?"

"We talked. We're good. We get along. It will work out."

"That's a relief. He didn't think you looked a little too..." Serena must choose her words carefully.

"Sectarian...."

"Nice choice of words, Hana." Serena raises her wine glass into the air.

"He likes me. Apparently, I was calling him 'Holy Father' and 'Great Holiness'."

"You didn't do that?"

"I didn't notice."

"Oh God. He might fire you now."

"Mother! Stop it. He likes me and thinks we can hit some big numbers with the Twitter account."

"Was it Cardinal Peter who mentioned how you were addressing the Holy Father?"

"Yes."

"I've always told you... if you bump into His Holiness on a bus..."

"Mother, please, don't embarrass me in front of Hana."

"Hana is fine!"

"Can you pour her a drink, please?!"

They break out in giggles. They hold each other's shoulders, or clutch their sides, to keep from laughing.

Serena sits on the stoop and reads her novel (Gabriel García Márquez's *One Hundred Years of Solitude*, the Italian translation). But Marco knows her routine all too well, and truthfully, she is waiting for Aldo to come over and drop off her "monthly allowance".

He does not transfer the funds electronically into her account, because Serena needs to feel the money. Aldo is a technological luddite, and he doesn't trust banks. Neither one will let it go. The problem, however, is much deeper than that. Aldo assumes a larger-than-life role in Serena's life, whether she likes it or not. Serena has become dependent on her brother. Marco has grown up within a sphere of male domination; Marco is the only one who describes the arrangement as abusive.

Aldo runs Serena off the side of a highway. Or she puts rat poison in the crepe mix. Serena has three ex boyfriends who have gone missing. Marco asks whether confronting his uncle is really worth it? Aldo drops the money off dutifully and even offers financial counselling.

Aldo visits the grocer's and pays her bills. And whenever Serena asks for some extra money to, say, go on a vacation, she always gets the same response: "My pool is how we define vacation."

There will be wedding bells, a white gown, and a swarthy man in a tux someday; at least this is what she tells herself. Personal freedom is not part of the family dynamic. Only after Aldo gets dementia from all the abuse his wife and Serena have inflicted upon him; then Serena can choose what she wants to do. But whatever choice she makes, Aldo maintains, will be far worse than anything even Aldo has dished out.

A large window overlooks the courtyard. Prints of Pope Faustino adorn the walls. One color print shows His Holiness at the White House.

Cardinal Peter looks inside the doorway.

"His Holiness says you misquoted him in our last post."

A swallow skids as he lands on the cement mantle.

His Holiness finds just being with someone outside his circle allows for a certain amount of playful entertainment. Marco will feign ignorance to make His Holiness feel as comfortable as possible. One time, His Holiness asks if perhaps they should go downstairs and have him sit on a motorcycle. His Holiness could sit on a Ducati, or maybe a Laverda. As His Holiness recalls his youth, he could race around a track sitting on a MV Augusta.

The motorcycle manufacturers would inevitably try and use the image to sell their wares.

An even better idea would be to have His Holiness wear a jersey that says "Pope Faustino" on the back. But

Pope Faustino won't have it, adding that he must not interfere with fair play. And besides, if God were able to let him tamper with the score, Argentina would win each game by several hundred goals.

"You would be willing to humiliate the opponent?"

"Of course, to show them the strength of God's power. Just a little reminder. Just a few hundred goals."

In your domestic life, you must take advantage of all of the resources to get clean. Get a girlfriend or a boyfriend, get married, start a family. In other words, the domestic life is where you are going to set yourself free, where you can really soar and find your personal happiness.

The job is not a story. We take the best advice from the most successful players and build on their expertise. But in domestic affairs, your mental health demands an open book when it comes to succeeding. But when the job comes, life and death is never more on the table.

"Did Pope Faustino ever play professional soccer when he was younger?"

"No, Marco. He has dedicated himself to the Lord, ever since he was very young."

Occasionally, you will meet other players, and they will try and distract you by discussing a job.

There are, of course, persons in the history of the Book who stand out.

Let us examine the life of Ned Kelly. He was born in the middle of the 19th century in Victoria, Australia. He was not your typical gangster. He would rob farms, take horses, and then warn the farm hands that he will be coming back in a couple of weeks. He would then add that they should make sure the pigs are well fed, as he wants to lock a better pay day when he makes the re-sale deal.

His biggest mistake, however, was the time he killed a police officer. I don't care if you are from Vancouver, Kalamazoo, or Timbuctoo, the moment you kill a cop, your life is over.

But, being in the middle of a job, things can get pretty exciting. Your eyeballs start to sweat, your breathing changes, and you don't know right from wrong. The job got the best of him. Dan Kelly, Ned's brother, was in the process of stealing a couple of horses when he was stopped by the police. Suddenly, Ned showed up. Big brother got into a kerfuffle with the police, his gun went off, and suddenly we had one dead cop.

The moment he tried to help his brother, he lost the privilege to live. He was no longer the inconspicuous gangster, plotting his next bank job. He was the leading man in world affairs, the target of considerable surveillance. And the surveillance was alerting everyone to join, to find Ned Kelly, and kill him.

The two brothers eventually created the Kelly Gang, and they earned quite the reputation. They were known as the Robin Hood of gangs, always interested in helping out the working man. Their story sold a lot of newspapers. But it did little to ease Ned's peace of mind.

Ned Kelly could have been one of the most powerful gangsters of all time. He was in a perfect place to launch an incredible career. His gang was feared all over Australia, Europe, and even the USA. I needn't remind you, during the depression, back in the USA gangster culture was making a name for itself due to the prohibition laws. We made a lot of money selling booze under the table.

One of our first rules is never stop a police officer from doing his job. It is one thing if you are on a job, and you are surrounded by cops. You are welcome to go out blazing. But don't do what Ned Kelly did – namely interfere while his brother was getting arrested – and think you are playing the hero.

Some might argue that Ned's brother represented an economic asset, and so he had a right to interfere. That might be true, but there is good word that Dan Kelly would have been out of jail in just a few days.

Suddenly, the entire Australian Army was after two fugitives. The military had to turn down volunteers from other countries, who wanted to bring Ned Kelly down.

The police were after Ned Kelly as a means to an end, rather than just doing their job. The police cannot sleep at night when the likes of Ned Kelley are alive. He was different from some regular Joe needing to rip off a bank. He wanted the police out of the story completely. As far as the police were concerned, Ned Kelly was a cop killer. And cop killers are not gangsters.

The editors meet twice per year, at some undisclosed location. They all take commercial flights to their destination, but the choice of location is not determined until they each arrive at the airport. Thereupon we run an algorithm to determine which city is the most logical destination based on ticket availability.

Often, it is a city in central Europe; however, we have hosted meetings in Warsaw and once in the Middle East. We tend to avoid the Middle East for security reasons. If, for example, one of our editors gets arrested and they are in the Middle East, it could get a little hairy to try and get them out. Plus, the cost of a legal team in the Middle East is off-the-charts expensive.

Each year, the editors go over all the petitions to add new gangsters into the Book. It is worth noting that, because there are so many jobs, we cannot include everyone's name. We go over each proposal with a fine-tooth comb. We review the risks involved while performing a job. And then we decide as a group whether or not to publish them.

We've had scenarios where a gangster has performed a heist, and then held on to the loot before they found a buyer. The waiting game can be very taxing on a gangster. We usually will give a one-year pass on publishing information about a heist. But the next year, regardless of whether the loot has been laundered, we will publish the findings.

We want the world to see what kinds of jobs are being done. Like we've said before, we see the merit in publishing this information because it demystifies the role of the gangster. But it also promotes our side of the story, which we think needs to be improved. We are showing the world that not everyone is perfect, and that hard-working gangsters are making a go at it in creative ways. Sometimes this brand of creativity makes for a great screenplay.

Our editors are not writers. They are merely interested in showing the world what has happened recently and making the person who committed a crime look a little more saintly than before.

Recently, we have been at loggerheads with many of the big-name crime families around the world. Of course, because we have no physical location, they cannot send us anything. If that were the case, we could probably bankroll our entire operation on bribes. That being said, there is a lot of interest in being published in the Book.

We have been asked to include pictures. We have decided to omit this kind of media because we don't like photography. The reason is because the history of photography has always portrayed criminals in a negative way. For example, think of the thousands of mugshots the public has seen of criminals over the years. Or else, a body lying in a pool of blood, a sheet covering a dead body on the street. Or some of our favorite: police officers and firemen standing in front of a scene of a crime, acting casual as though they should feel proud standing at the scene of a crime. In other words, the criminal world cannot accept the ways in which photojournalism has treated us. But it is more than unfair treatment: photojournalism has created a monolith whereby criminals are always seen portrayed in a bad light. The unfair juxtaposition does not help the general public understand the real meaning of a criminal. Indeed, the media's portrayal perpetuates a myth that criminals are dark, salacious, or deadbeats, when none of that is true. We are, however, open to cinematic portrayals or biopics, because they tend to nail our portrayals to perfection. Of course, we have our hands full making sure the scripts are properly written before they hit the big screen.

Another inquiry relates to war crimes. We have seen examples of genocide, with an untold number of people who have died, and lots of these are different from the kinds of crimes that regular gangsters are engaged in.

I once received an email from a well-known diamond thief from Mexico who was very learned in the Frankfurt

School. He explained to us that there have been countless Marxist revolutions that have raged in south and central America, and from these lengthy and impressive battles, numerous criminal organizations have sprung. It also happened in Russia, during the 1990s, when gangsterism was at its peak. However, these criminal gangs are the by-product of political instability. And in that sense their wealth is built on the backs of the citizenry. It is not to say that these kinds of criminal organizations are not impressive or intimidating, but their influence is somewhat limited insofar as their first steps into the criminal lands were due to some political situation.

Don't get us wrong, we like our friends in every part of the world, but when it comes to ensuring the Book's everlasting quality, we must draw a line in the sand.

The other request we often see is this business surrounding mass murders. Mass murder is a prickly issue for lots of reasons. First of all, a mass murderer is unstable to begin with. He is usually a psychopath, and this is usually combined with a multitude of imaginary happenings going on in his head. These people will sometimes cling to a political cause, or else be excessively anti-government or anti-institution.

There is no financial gain in mass murder. Not to mention the constant slew of death threats. The mass murderer weakens America's reputation around the world and alienates people and cultural institutions within the USA.

From our perspective, the mass murderer is ultimately seen as a disease. There is a man who has lost all of his desire to be nice. He sees no value in simple conversations. It is a hyperactive man, who likes to hold his gun. And we find this strange because a gun is an awkward sort of thing to hold. But the mass murderer seems to think that a gun somehow reflects leisure and joy and freedom. We know this is completely false: a gun is cumbersome and silly-looking.

And somehow the mass murder has fed the idea that it feels good to unload an automatic. We always say: turn on the microwave. Or else, turn on a stove and watch the burner turn red. TV is good. There is nothing cathartic about a gun releasing bullets. It is plain stupid.

There is also the child mass murderer, which I will not address, because we really don't understand what would prompt a child to do such a thing. The questions are relevant, and hopefully our philosophers and psychologists will attempt to seek answers to this line of questioning, especially the high number of children who commit suicide, because this is reaching alarming levels.

The final bit on the table is Martyrdom. We get lots of these kinds of requests. To be frank, their arguments for inclusion tend to be much more interesting than those of the mass murderer, but we still refuse their petitions. The simple reason is that we do not have sufficient information about the Kingdom of God. If it could be shown that the Kingdom of God does include great riches, then we would be more interested in continuing the conversation. But, so far, no one has been able to convince us about the riches of the Kingdom of God. We need to be able to enter the Kingdom of God, check out the place, make sure we can see a clean escape route, and then, maybe, we'll entertain some ideas of including some of these characters in the Book. For now, the answer is "no".

Marco sits on the bench. The subway platform overflows with crowds. He gawks at the tourists. He feels no different from some Midtown Manhattan advertising executive, the one who decides which adverts to put inside *Rolling Stone*, *Vogue*, or *Time*. And yet, His Holiness makes the Twitter account feel as though it is quite dissimilar from all those things. Cardinal Peter is interested in understanding the Twitter account as a vehicle to communicate His Holiness's popularity. There is an undeniable acceptance about the quantitative value of His Holiness's popularity.

His Holiness promises that, upon reaching a certain number of Catholics, they will celebrate God's reach. And now, Marco is asked to speculate on what differences lie at the heart of the large number of followers.

"If some of those people are simply going to the beach to cool off, how difficult might it be to ask them to look up at the heavenly skies and see Christ come into their heart?"

As he thinks back to his time at the technology conference in Boulder, studying the latest MIS designs or computer language, he cannot help but be disappointed in all the time he wasted in the classroom. The Vatican teaches its employees what they have to know.

It should be noted that Cardinal Peter is scheming to turn social media on its head. He only teaches what you need to know, namely that His Holiness is a special character, different from the shopkeeper down the street. A no-brainer, but that is the kind of logic he likes to push.

"We must be respectful of Messi, as he is an Argentine, but, recall, only one person wins the Tour de France."

He looks out the window at great distances and laughs. Never at His Holiness, but at his wry sense of humour. These are not racy jokes, launched from some seedy comedy stage, which Marco and Hana visited in Boulder. These are little turns of phrase which are humorous only when stated quickly. And His Holiness will dilute his humour with some banal observation, like the sound of church bells in the distance, or ordering one of his staff to get him a cup of coffee. In other words, His Holiness's natural gifts for humour are invariably eviscerated by his tenure as Pope. The outcome makes one miss the occasional laugh, but later, seated at his desk, Marco is known to fall on the floor.

The changes are subtle, but there are signs that a new dynamic is emerging within the family. For example, Aldo, who typically hosts family gatherings at his house, inquires if they can dine near the Vatican.

Marco finishes his toast to the bride, when suddenly Aldo rises up from his chair and asks Marco if His Holiness will be hosting the wedding ceremony.

"What are you talking about?"

"Is Pope Faustino going to marry you?"

Serena goes over to Aldo and puts her arms around his thick, hairy neck. She whispers that His Holiness does not preside over weddings. Marco will be lucky if he can get the day off.

"But I thought His Holiness was your friend?"

"No!"

"You've been working with this man for four months, and you've made him more famous. And he won't attend your wedding?"

"You're not making any sense."

"But it would be good for the family business. You know, like in *The Godfather*."

Marco reaches over and asks if he can speak to Hana alone.

"I don't want to give you the wrong impression, but I will not be able to introduce your father to His Holiness."

"I know."

"OK. I feel very bad about this. I mean, my own mother, too. It's nothing personal."

Marco can hear Hirato in the background.

"My father is not Catholic."

"Oh?"

"Yes, he likes that you work for him, but for him it's all about status."

Hana rushes back to her iPad and continues to make arrangements with her dad. Midori will remain in Tokyo and take care of Naomi.

During a commonplace exchange with a client, the client accused Naomi of being racist. Naomi was flabbergasted at the accusation. She is part Korean, and the accusation felt like a total insult, compounded by the fact that it was not true. Naomi told the client that her opinion was non-sensical. However, her response was the incorrect one, and the claim of racism stands. A long chain of conversations ensued between the client and her husband and two highly careerist managers who tried to defend Naomi as best they could. However, they reported back to Naomi each mid-morning for over a week, saying they continued to talk to the client, and she maintained that Naomi is a racist and that Naomi should be fired. Furthermore, the client then said she was thinking of going to the press. Naomi is in fear of reprisal, and now requires around-the-clock attention. A doctor admits the crying is highly unusual. It is caused by depression and not anything in particular at the bank.

"If she stops crying, she will start to feel better."

Marco puts Hirato's belongings into the car, and motions for Hana and Hirato to get in. Hana warns Marco that her dad will use the plane ride as an excuse to get drunk. And true to her word, Hirato appears a little white.

He acts like the shuttle bus driver back in Boulder, who has thick arms and points at different landmarks, distancing traffic. Marco even darts quick glances at Hana and at the back seat. Hirato is snoring, or else, moments later, he has his neck tilted backwards and looks out the window, and yelps "Eiffel Tower next stop." Hana smacks Marco on the knee. As they approach the apartment, there is a feeling of growing domesticity. The feeling is even more pronounced when Marco offers to carry Hirato up the stairs.

Diego rolls his eyes at the new guest and rushes into his apartment. Serena stands in the kitchen and pours a tall glass of wine. Hirato slumps down on the couch and passes out. Serena reassures Marco that she will be OK: these are friends who are going to finally help her become independent.

"How is that possible?"

"Because we meet at an AA meeting."

Marco enters the kitchen with two empty bottles of red wine. He holds them in the air like he is a downhill skier catching air at death-defying speeds.

"You're just jealous I'm developing a social life."

"I've got a social life."

"What are you talking about, not like mine?"

"Look around."

Suddenly, Hirato raises his head from the couch and motions for Serena to come over. Serena goes over to Hirato, whereupon he lightly taps her knee and points at the window.

"When are we landing?"

Inside the social media offices, Marco finds a note from His Holiness. The note reads:

Please meet me in the garden as I want to discuss strategy for boosting the Twitter numbers.

Cardinal Peter meets Marco in the hallway before he is about to go outside.

"What are you doing?"

"I'm meeting the Holy Father in the garden, like he requested."

"What?"

"There was a note on my desk."

"The Holy Father has never set foot in our offices. Why would he do that?"

"You are wise, but you cannot see all things. He left me a note."

Cardinal Peter takes the reigns and tries to prepare Marco the best he can.

"Just act polite and smile and show him you like your job."

"OK."

Marco walks away. Cardinal Peter thinks to himself: I'm more puzzled by this man than the question of who is going to be the next Pope.

The Vatican Gardens are a mix of Italian, English, and French style garden. There is a mixture of paths and sculptures and fountains, with influences from the Italian Renaissance and the Baroque school. It even includes some caves and several smallish temples. It is famous for the grotto of the Madonna della Guardia.

His Holiness greets Marco. They sit on a bench.

"I quite like just sitting in these gardens."

"I can see why. They are rather impressive."

"We've maintained these gardens since the Middle Ages."

Pope Faustino knows that Marco was a little bit unsure about their meeting.

"Around the 15th century. I don't know the name of the gardener, but he did a marvelous job."

"I could find out. I can ask Cardinal Peter."

"Are you referring to the gardener who worked here six hundred years ago?"

"I can still ask if you like?"

"We need to review our messages. Let me read something to you: 'May you always experience the joy that comes from putting Christ in your heart'."

Marco remains quiet. And now it is too late. His Holiness continues to wait for his response.

"That is the message I jotted down when they asked me to send a message to our followers, back in 2012."

"Very impressive. I'm surprised you can recall your first Tweet. I can hardly remember what I ate for breakfast this morning."

"Marco, I can see you are beginning to relax in front of me."

"Of course."

"Not 'of course'. Don't forget that not very long ago

you were a nervous nelly. I had to carry our conversations like I was holding the cross for the both of us."

"I never noticed. I'm sorry."

Serena ties a napkin around Hirato's neck. She slams her hand on the table, and then reorients herself in front of Hirato and neatly tucks the napkin under his collar. Next, she goes around the table and points the wooden spoon at Marco, who is a little startled by the attention.

"You are not supposed to eat just whenever you want."

"Give me a break."

"You give me a break. We have guests, and they come from great distances. The least you can do is show a little bit of respect and be polite."

Hana gives an embarrassed look at her father. Marco peers at Hirato, who looks stately, but also a little apprehensive, with some of the same feelings Marco felt while in Japan. The conversation feels rickety. Hirato remains silent. Hana is uncertain about her father's train of thought, and Serena offers the perfect amount of respect to make him feel part of the family.

After Serena serves dessert (two kinds of ice cream), and just as Marco places the spoon to his lips, Serena screams: "Giorgio is dead!"

Marco's and Hirato's eyes meet. Marco nods with disapproval as though to say Giorgio's death will have a horrible impact on all their lives. Hirato stands up and points at the night sky full of stars: "God bless you, Giorgio."

Serena curses under her breath and looks at Marco, who is in a state of shock. Serena, with pursed lips, motions for Marco to calm down.

Rumours circulate that he died from suicide. Giorgio comes from a good Catholic family. His family cannot accept suicide as the cause of death. Indeed, the revised obituary, which was written by Giorgio's sister, Bianca, who owns a Greek catering business, gives the impression that Giorgio was recently reborn. Serena attends the funeral and returns home in shock: she hardly recognized the man who was discussed at the funeral. Despite the break-up, Serena is under the spell that her life is inextricably linked to Giorgio's death. The little bit of tenderness that Serena and Giorgio shared makes her think twice about her own mortality.

Her sense of mischief gets the better of her. And now she finds it hard to dislodge thoughts of murder. She is convinced Aldo is responsible. She wrestles with how she is going to find the truth.

She stays up all hours of the night and cries and intends to revenge his death. She has stopped talking to Aldo. She tells Marco that if he continues to have a relationship with his uncle, she will disown him. Hana spends hours listening to Serena, and then she'll repeat the stories back to her father. Hirato finds the situation very complicated, because back home in Japan, the male tends to hold an inordinate amount of power around the table. And now he is witnessing first-hand the power of Serena's sorrow. She sits on her knees in the middle of the hallway, blocking anyone from accessing the washroom. If one did not get up early in the morning, one might be trapped in their room, unable to access the bathroom.

Serena feels she is entitled to let herself go. She is

ignorant of how she presents herself inside the apartment. She often uses Marco and Hana and Hirato to try and better understand why she is so emotional. And then, one day, it dawns on her, that she has stopped grieving.

We have seen examples where domestics have become too wayward in their life. Just remember, we recommend you build a cover, but, at the end of the day, when you get the call for your next job, we become your primary focus. We have seen examples of domestics who have become stronger because they are so deep in their cover. Whatever you do, never equate your domestic life as reality. We have seen domestics fall for their domestic life, and then as soon as we ask for a favor, they act strange. Don't set yourself up for a disaster.

They sit in the living room. Serena drinks an *aperitivo*. Marco is scared because he knows, deep down, he can never face his uncle. Serena expects Marco to say all the right things. Finally, Marco offers to kill his uncle. Or else, they'll hire an investigator and build a case. He sees the grave burden she holds for her family. She smiles at Marco upon seeing this recognition on his face. And now, Marco is clueless about how to approach the situation.

The burden of the family is too powerful a force on his mother's face, and despite her acceptance, she wears their misfortunes (disgust) with tenor, poise, and episodic beauty. It becomes too much for Marco. Of course, these are the implications of a dysfunctional family. More often than not, their reactions are gestures of disgust and scornful chuckles, because all of the tenderness of love has been snipped away in favor of criminal tendencies.

"You should stop thinking so much."

"What do you mean?"

They choose to go to Denny's and have breakfast in the middle of the day. Suddenly, they find themselves under fire for taking a booth when a family was waiting in line ahead of them ("they could have sat at the counter," yelps the little girl). And suddenly Marco and Hana can finally live their life in peace. And Marco looks over the table, and takes Hana's hand, and kisses her on the forehead.

"I mean, you have the look of a thousand deaths. And yet you work with Father Almighty himself."

"Oh, that is nothing. His Holiness cannot change who I am as a person, and if I see that you are suffering so much, I must try and help."

"Giorgio was a man with problems like everybody. But he did not deserve to die."

"What are you asking me to do here, Ma?"

"I'm not asking you to do anything."

Marco gets up from his chair and goes over to the window. Aldo parks the car. He looks straight up at his sister's apartment. He holds his gaze on his nephew. His giant steps put fear into the entire building.

Aldo acts as though he has never been there before. Serena does not move. She holds her eyes on Marco. Marco glances at his uncle but offers no invitation to speak. Somehow, Aldo knows that is an invitation for him to be himself and try and help. Aldo feels invigorated. His family stands a chance. But he doesn't know what that means exactly. Serena gets up from the couch and goes into the kitchen.

The Vatican is not recognized by the UN, but the Holy

See is recognized by the Assembly General. The Holy See administers all the religious buildings throughout Rome. And each building holds immunity from Italian law.

Serena continues to drink her aperitivo, and ignores Aldo, who is paralyzed with fear. Things do not improve when Marco makes the mistake of mentioning Napoli in the standings.

The problem with Aldo's rationalisations is that there are so many ways of fabricating some unloving story about Serena. Because his imagination is so wild and disturbing, he is empowered by his own paranoia. He is so indecent as to voice these fabrications to anyone who will listen; he can barely come up for air before he is criticized for his rude behaviour.

"Napoli always play well because they once had Maradona."

"But that's different. That is the past."

"Yes, that is the past."

Marco enters the kitchen and returns with a plate of anginetti, glazed lemon knots. He places them on the coffee table. Aldo politely reaches over and places a couple of sweets on a napkin. Marco takes a sip of his cappuccino. The lines are clearly defined, and Giorgio is not going to be mentioned. Aldo has already come up with a reasonable excuse and will make Serena and Marco look silly.

His hairy arms come over her curved back. Instinctively she dislikes the attention, and she tries to escape the hug, his two, three rolls of blubber neatly hanging over his double pleated pants.

Marco is full of shame. But it is a different feeling than before, and regardless of whether Aldo is responsible for Giorgio's death, everyone feels relieved about the meeting.

Hana translates the television reports. Marco goes to the website every day and checks for updates. People are scared. They don't know what to believe. The difficulty lies in the fact that the WHO only releases a news update once per day. All sorts of conspiracy theories emerge.

Hirato is convinced that COVID-19 was invented by the Chinese government to overthrow the world. And yet, rather paradoxically, the solution lies in moving to China, where everyone will be safe from the pandemic.

Marco insists they travel outside the city, and just take a break from everything. Serena has just finished being under very close watch for several months. Now that she is refreshed (Aldo thinks she's turned over a new leaf and might even work someday), she can watch Hirato, perhaps even transition him from conspiracist back to the real world.

The major news stations cover the terrorist attack as tastefully as possible. Psychologists are brought in to help the hotel employees deal with the situation.

A news reporter finds one of our agents, who is more than willing to give an interview (that is what he is trained to do). A blind man stands at the back of the theatre, surrounded by a group of men considerably taller than him. And there is a little kerfuffle on the stage. And suddenly the blind man is asked what he sees.

His Holiness is miffed about Marco's decision to take

a leave of absence.

"You know, in times of crisis, we must all try and be strong, and not just run away."

"I want to show my girlfriend some of the Italy that I remember as a child."

"That's very well, but who is going to take care of me?"

"Cardinal Peter mentioned to me that it will be taken care of."

"You know, I pray for that man to stop smoking more than I can tell you. I'm going to give myself lung cancer if I pray for him anymore. And you're sure he knows how to use Twitter?"

"Of course."

"I sense that you're searching for the right things, and I want you to have this time for yourself."

Cardinal Peter asks him why he needs time off. Marco is speechless: he cannot tell his boss his girlfriend's father suffers illusions. Or that he only speaks Japanese. His Holiness insists that Marco will take up his role as digital expert when he returns.

Hirato likes to eat a simple breakfast. In the afternoons, he mostly reads or surfs the net. But the latter should be discouraged due to his obsessive-compulsive tendencies. He enjoys long walks or else he likes to go out shopping.

Road trip

Aldo comes over to drop off some groceries. Hirato has been playing online poker for nine days, while sitting on the kitchen floor in jeans and no shirt, with a continuous murmur and occasional sensible conversation with himself. The recognition of each other's existence only happens when Hirato loses a hand, and almost destroys his iPhone.

It is fair game to walk away, to visit another room, and shake off his visit with Hirato, like leaving a room full of David Hammond works of art.

"Is this the little man who used to live here?"

"He still lives here?"

"He's planning on moving to China. Don't worry about him."

The plastic bag appears to rip just as Aldo places it on the counter. Serena opens the peanut butter and makes a sandwich. Aldo admits he is worried by all the news stories. It is the first time Serena has seen a vulnerable side to him. And what's more, he is not ranting about the suspicious origins of the disease. Instead, he acts detached and a little fatalistic. Aldo adds that Marco should not have gone on holiday at such a precarious time. The conversation cascades into a non-sensical argument about how Marco should have remained behind so he could keep the family in the loop about the Church's position on COVID-19.

"He's coming back eventually."

"We'll all be dead."

"Come on, you came over here, dropped off groceries, and thank you, but now you're saying all sorts of mean things."

"No, I just think it would be nice to have some muscle inside the Vatican at a time like this so we can be in the know when the Armageddon happens."

"We're all going to die, Serena. Don't you get it!"

Serena stands in the kitchen and focusses on Marco.

The conversation started off well enough, but it has spilled into conspiracy theory. And then, suddenly, Hirato rushes into the kitchen and screams: "ten thousand euros!" The walls shake, the runway carpet flops over, and then naked feet smack on the hardwood floor, and there are yelps of sheer joy.

"You won?"

"Yes!!"

Marco wants to see Switzerland. They visit northern Italy instead. Yet, the geography neither compliments a vacation destination, nor helps soothe the original intentions as to why they went away in the first place.

They stop in a little town. They exit the pharmacy and put on their masks. They have trouble speaking.

The moment of truth happens when Hana leaves the bank. And she looks at the bank receipt and it says "two million dollars".

His Holiness does not see joy in the world. He sees human suffering. The joys, Marco repeats, do not exist. Where is the joy? Marco searches more and more for clues. He looks around the room. He searches the eyes of His Holiness. Diego is at the side of the room playing with the soccer ball. He feels the intimidation of his faith.

He can feel the weight of his mother's stare.

They are not aware of the legal reasons why they must wear a mask. And then there are some who wear their masks because they are asked to wear them by someone else. These people tend to act lazily and their masks slouch or do not cover their noses. Or else, they wear it around their chin, which makes it look like they have a beard.

They sit inside the hotel room and watch the news. Marco wiggles his hands in the air as he speaks. Hana gets in the habit of smacking Marco's leg. She watches the news from Japan on her iPad.

"We are going to die. And we never got married."

Marco leans against his Peugeot and snuggles Hana close to him. He stretches his hand into the air and takes a selfie with Hana in his arms. Marco uploads the picture to Instagram. They return to the hotel room. Marco opens the smoked salmon and cuts it into small chunks and adds it to the rice bowl.

There is nothing to do as the stores and restaurants are all closed. They sit for a time in a park. Back at the hotel, they sit on the bouncy bed, with empty, modern bookshelves and fake plants, and talk until they need to get up and stretch. Hana spends an inordinate amount of time thanking Marco for helping her father. But they end up laughing at her appreciation, because it is something anyone would do. Marco listens as she snores. At 4 am, there is a knock at the door.

The blinds have metal strips, and the string to raise them is not working. As Marco pushes at the sides, the metal scrapes against the window.

The lights are difficult to find, a humming TV, and

now he stands in the shoe tray, and he jogs on the spot to get clean.

Finally, he rips open the thick door, which has the action of a modern refrigerator. Somehow, despite a good dosage of fear, he raises his eyebrows, and raises a hand with a pointed finger, and looks at the stranger straight in the eye.

The medical volunteer appears very professional in his uniform; he wears a full head to toe suit, with a red cross on his chest.

The stranger asks Marco some medical-related questions. And just as Marco becomes calm with their meeting, the man asks Marco for one hundred euros. The money, the stranger explains, is a city tax for providing residents with life-saving medical advice.

"I don't understand. What is your title?"

"Listen, I'm trying to help you. Don't be so indignant and resentful. Just give me some money."

Hana decides to see what the commotion is all about. First, she fixes the blinds, turns off the TV, she even empties the shoe tray of water, and then goes on the balcony and searches for Marco.

"Listen man, you are going to die, just let me help you."

A little bit of jeering back and forth follows. The hotel manager appears and the fighting stops. The manager pushes the man down the cement staircase, and then across the parking lot. And in the sparring, it is revealed that the manager knows the man.

If someone else answered the door, who had no pact with Aldo, they would have dealt with the stranger accordingly. And yet, Marco's disposition encourages the stranger to make up some outlandish story.

"But he could have killed you. And little me."

Marco stares at the popcorn ceiling, and gently glides his leg against Hana's soft leg. Her body is perfect. And they both contemplate making love, which lasts for several more hours. Finally, Marco awakens. He goes out to the balcony where he is met by a group of hotel guests coming down the balcony. A little boy rushes towards Marco.

"Are you immune from the disease?"

"No, why?"

"Well, you're not wearing a mask."

"He's smarter than I was at that age."

"Diseases make people smart. And I'm only seven."

The small dining room is decorated with F1 posters in expensive poster frames. There is even a picture of Alberto Tomba on black felt, which is probably worth a small fortune. A small table is pushed against the wall: an expresso machine, toaster, microwave, containers with dry cereal, and raison bread, already buttered.

The hotel manager wakes up with a zest for life he has never felt before.

He cannot stop thinking of Marco. For it is Marco that somehow triggers this eternal breath to come out of his body.

His hands are scraped from falling down the stairs. Indeed, he cannot stop saying he intends to kill Emiliano.

When it comes to exchanging pleasantries with Marco, his eyes begin to swell with tears. And immediately he feels intimidated. And he lets go of all the solemn feelings, and immediately drops his "fake feelings", which gives Marco the chance to leave in peace.

The hotel manager speaks quickly and acts dismissive towards Hana. He talks in a way that makes it very hard for Marco to look at Hana and explain what is going on. The police visit shops in the neighborhood and interview the guests. It turns out, Emiliano, the man who was asking for money, used to work at the front desk.

"We're leaving."

"Why?"

"Because I don't like what I'm becoming in this place."

The hotel manager has somehow forgiven Emiliano. And it is plain to Marco that the manager recognizes that his feelings are the wrong ones. What's more, Marco wants revenge, and it takes all of his being to show this indifference, but the manager is bothered by the look in Marco's eyes. And he cannot stand being with this man for very much longer.

"Here, take these masks. You might need them."

They arrive at Crema. There is an unmistakeable silence in the air. They are surrounded by ambulances on all sides. At the intersection, there is a traffic jam with one ambulance trying to get around another ambulance.

"It makes the city look even more beautiful."

"What?"

"I mean, all the ambulances remind me of death, and it seems more beautiful against the Italian buildings."

The owner of the shop wears a mask and ski goggles and looks like a giant insect. In grubby green corduroys, he stares at the burning cigar rolling on the sidewalk.

He instructs Marco to pull up his mask, and then blocks Hana from going inside. Hana is only allowed to enter thirty seconds after Marco enters the store. But they are not allowed to stand beside each other once they are inside the store.

"But she doesn't speak Italian, and she'll need my help."

"I lost a brother yesterday from the Chinese disease, so you can suck my tit."

Marco looks at Hana and motions for her to return to the car.

Aldo calls Marco using FaceTime.

"It appears that the old man has begun drinking again, and now he wants to go home."

"He doesn't speak Italian, and you speak worse English than he does."

Hana calls her dad. He answers the phone. He is watching a movie. And hangs up.

"What in the hell is going on?"

"Nothing out of the usual. Except the airlines have stopped flying back to Japan, and so now I'm looking into becoming an Italian citizen, because they've taken away my right to return to our country. And I intend to get very drunk."

"You sound very drunk already."

There was a long pause before Hirato answered again.

"Aldo made pasta last night, and I think he should open a restaurant."

Marco asks for the phone and politely asks Hirato if he can speak to his mother.

They end up speaking for some time. Of course, Serena is fully aware of the medical emergency in Crema. And the numbers are getting higher with each passing day. Serena pleads with Marco to come home.

He feels shame at how intelligent she sounds. It could have been a nurse or a doctor. But instead, she acts dismissive about the world and careers, because Aldo has convinced her that professions are not important. She begins to scream when she notices Hirato has spilled a glass of wine on the carpet. She forgets to come back to the phone. She repeats that she refuses to be anyone's grandmother if Hirato does not get his shit together. She goes on a long diatribe about the risks of having sex during COVID-19. Marco apologizes that he called, and promises to wear a mask, social distance, and wash his hands with anti-bacterial solutions. Serena hangs up the phone before he can finish.

Serena no longer enjoys making supper for Hirato each night. She serves *Trippa alla Romana*, which is tripe in tomato sauce and mint and pecorino cheese, and Hirato simply does not understand what he is being served. And Serena refuses to defend Italian cuisine. She no longer enjoys sitting in the TV room and watching a movie with Hirato. He tends to remain quiet, and then speaks for very long stretches about Japan, even though she doesn't understand a single word he is saying. Or he mumbles something from the hallway as though they had just had a great connection. It borders on mental abuse. She is overcome with shame and embarrassment. He nods politely when he is ready to eat and enjoys saying "thank you very much." Or his favorite: "you are too kind to me."

The Vatican

Marco presents his mom with several gifts. Hana presents her dad with even more gifts.

The fancy paper makes Serena look twice. She thinks it is probably a box of Italian chocolates or mints. But it turns out they are rose-shaped soaps.

Hirato is given a deck of playing cards, among other things, which triggers a long, worried look from Serena, who thinks Hirato needs to slow down with the gambling.

Serena reflects upon her time growing up: I was just a little girl when I learned about my role. At one time, I had my father, Sylvester, and Aldo against the ropes. And then my father died, and Aldo suddenly felt he owned the family. He lost control of his senses. There was a time when I could have run, where the streets had names. Instead, I met a guy, a made guy, and we started a family. He owned laundromats. I had Marco. My job was very simple: most days I would go to the few shops around Rome and pick up the change. We made enough money to cover the rent. We went to Athens on our second wedding anniversary. He went away on business, where he claimed he was looking for locations. And then I saw him on the nightly news, in a pool of blood at a bank robbery in Paris.

"In Paris?! And he thought a trip to Athens was supposed to be romantic?"

"His friends got away with twenty million euros. Meanwhile, he was lying in a pool of gasoline and blood with a bullet hole in the side of the head?!"

"I waited until Marco was ten before I told him how his father died."

Sylvester, Serena's father, had just completed training to work as a dispatcher when he got a call from a middleman in the neighborhood and offered a job.

The deal was very straightforward: he was required to take a kilo of heroin to a hotel in exchange for a duffle bag of money.

The exchange seemed easy enough. He was on the verge of landing a new job, and all the pressures from home (his newly pregnant wife pleaded with him not to work with the mob because she did not want him killed), and he didn't really need the money. He wasn't even intimidated by the potential consequences of backing out. Accordingly, he bought into the plan, but he explained to his boss that this would be his last job. Everyone agreed. Sylvester was provided with a gun, and told the normal stuff, like if he tried to take the money and run, they would find him and break his legs and put a gun down his throat and twist the gun several times before they shoot. Sylvester was rather shocked by this last bit of description, to which his boss replied that he had had a few runners lately and they needed to make sure everyone understood they meant business.

The night before the plan was set to take place, Sylvester went out and had a few drinks at the local bar. Someone came up to him and sat down at the bar. He introduced himself as Fernando. Fernando must have been sixty or so. He was very tall. He could hardly sit down on the stool, because his knees seemed to kick into the air. He had grey hair which was tapered at the back.

The brill cream was off-putting, forcing Sylvester to hold his beer close to his face while he drank.

"I have to meet some guy tomorrow night and make a swap of money for some heroin. And I don't know if I should kill this motherfucker or not," Fernando said.

Sylvester took a sip of his beer and then reached over the counter and appeared to try and grab the Coke spray gun, when the bartender came over and removed the gun from his hand.

"What do you need, friend?"

"I think I'll buy my friend another round of whatever he's drinking, and I'll take a shot of your best tequila."

Sylvester lifted his drink, and Fernando took his scotch, and they shot their drinks back. Neither one spoke another word to the other.

Sylvester stepped off his stool and stood in the aisle behind the bar and looked towards the front, where a man in a white suit stood on a stage, with a red, velvet curtain backdrop. The man on stage waved at Sylvester as though they knew each other. It was the perfect opportunity to walk up to the musician and ask him questions like what songs he was intending to play, had he recorded, did he come here often? But instead, Sylvester went outside, and the night was mysterious, because it had not turned black. The sun shimmered behind the long, darkened streets. The memories of the day were ripe, or else a friendly acceptance that night had settled, and it shimmered with a kind of permanence. Sylvester could see himself sitting at the bar for several more drinks and longer conversations.

But Sylvester had no connection with Fernando. Sylvester simply discarded his talk like refuse on the street. Like a can which could sometimes be kicked for a little longer than usual. "For I am not God," he said to himself, "what right do I have to interfere with someone who may or may not have killed another man? God is the only one who can interfere in such kinds of circumstances."

Sylvester lay down in bed and reached over and felt the leg of his wife, who was already half asleep. He listened to the sounds inside the small, cramped apartment, and he realized he had to get out. They needed a bigger apartment. A baby was on the way, and hopefully there would be more. He got up and fixed the drip from the kitchen sink. He sat down at the kitchen table and had a glass of red wine and smoked three cigarettes. Vanna would chirp a few solemn words to come back to bed. But he remained in the kitchen and worried and drank.

He rolled out of bed, and entered the kitchen as usual, with a perfunctory kiss on the side of his wife's face. He faced the kitchen table where there was a basket of bread and espresso already set out. He smiled but he had a lot on his mind, and he didn't want to speak very much. He knew she could pry it out of him if they got going on another banter. He remained an outsider, refusing to engage his wife, even spoiling breakfast, spilling his espresso on the clean, white, lace tablecloth.

The day was spent at the café up the street where he read the newspaper and played a few games of pool. Then, he went out for a short walk, eventually arriving at his brother's, where they mucked around on the balcony and barbecued rabbit and drank Portuguese beer.

He made up some excuse about why he had to leave. By now, it seemed everyone knew about the deal, but it was getting late. He kissed his brother on the cheek, gave him a bear hug, and ventured out into the night.

The street was dark and lonely. Everyone was acting sullen, children were screaming without any reason, dogs were being tugged at by their owners to walk faster. Something had come over everyone, and yet Sylvester wouldn't have any of it. He wrestled with his shirt sleeves as he walked. He even got into a shouting match with an older man on the street. A young man peered at Sylvester from the window, and he pointed at him holding a knife.

Sylvester climbed the stairs. He entered the room, just like he was instructed. He opened the briefcase and made sure all of the heroin was there. Next, he went to the window, and there was a kerfuffle on the street. He could see Fernando, but he was being harassed by the kid from the window. Next, Fernando took out a gun and shot the young man. He came barrelling up the stairs. Sylvester stared at the man from the bar. He pointed his gun at Sylvester and told him to put the heroin on the bed. Next, he tossed the briefcase of money on the bed.

"It's all there, but we have a dead boy on the street. But at least you get to live."

"This is how God wanted it."

"That's right, man. You get to live. But that's only because I messed up downstairs!"

"Just let me go!"

Fernando left the room and raced down the stairs. Sylvester followed a minute later.

Sylvester stood beside the young boy. An old man appeared, and looked at his son, and fell to his knees.

"You better get out of here. I know you didn't do anything. But just leave."

These are moments when Marco wants to come clean

about his time in Boulder. And his relationship with Hana. And the real fears that pervade his life. As he lays his eyes on his mom, and feels her warmth, she knows much clearer than anyone (more than His Holiness, and the sweat of building castles, and the pomp of order) that Marco has made a wrong turn. And now she prays for him. For she knows that Marco has to answer for what he has done. And she knows that she will survive.

"We are self-isolating."

"What does that mean?"

"That means we cannot allow guests into the house for safety reasons."

There is a long pause. And it is the sense of irony that prompts Aldo to look over his shoulder and search for the right words.

"But I want to isolate with you guys. I miss you."

"You don't understand, you can't. Go home to your wife and my niece and nephew."

"Serena, you're just avoiding me!"

"No, these are instructions from the government and I'm protecting your health. You'll thank me later."

Aldo has no sympathy for rules. Rules are made to be broken. Aldo has always distrusted the government. Lawyers are a necessary evil. The only reason he befriends lawyers is to learn of ways to cheat the system even more. He owns a moving company. And a real estate company, which is one of the worst kinds of business operation a quasi-mafia hood can get his hands on. He hosted an estate sale and earned good money. And suddenly, they are in constant need of finding new properties to host. And it sometimes requires Aldo to approach potential customers and ask them to offer up their property. Aldo finds a way to host an estate sale for someone who has no interest in hosting an estate sale. Aldo says he is a successful businessman.

The stuff Aldo is doing puts families on the street. It causes panic in small towns.

Serena asks Aldo to explain to his nephew why people in their thirties host an estate sale?

"That is normal."

He makes money for his customers. Aldo tries to hold a straight face. This is an on-going argument and tends to end when the lamps are thrown across the room. Aldo asserts he is a creative business owner and gifted at transforming society.

Suddenly, the Casina Pio IV is the centre of the universe. It acts as an independent think tank, with eighty independent scientists, appointed for life by His Holiness, to address questions of science.

They are under no obligation to His Holiness, or the Church for that matter, to divulge any specifics about their research. And now, Cardinal Peter is going back and forth, and suddenly the pressure to make sure the science aligns with Catholic reasoning is fresh on everyone's minds.

Cardinal Peter welcomes Marco at the front doors. Everyone is required to wear a mask.

"I half expected that you would never come back?"

"How so?"

Cardinal Peter drops his sense of not understanding why Marco went away when he did.

"I called your mother while you were away, you know?"

"She didn't say anything?"

"Because I told her not to tell you. We were checking up on you."

"We?"

"His Holiness was curious how you were doing. Of course, he needs to be very cautious with his health, and when he learned that you were in the Serrano, he almost had a heart attack."

"Why is my personal life so important to everyone? I am the most boring person in the world."

"No, you are the social media expert for His Holiness."

"I see."

"If he is asking questions about you – then I need to make sure you are doing the right things. And that means making sure you are in the right frame of mind."

"Never mind, Cardinal Peter."

His Holiness never enters this section of the Vatican. And yet he stands in the middle of the room, looking at all the pictures on the wall. He is preparing the troops. He acts as though social media is going to win the war.

Despite His Holiness's towering presence, Marco turns to Cardinal Peter. And suddenly, there are some unspoken words about the state everyone finds themselves in. And His Holiness, who is pious and disciplined in his thinking, cannot help but feel a little jittery about his resources. He knows all of the ideas discussed at the Casina Pio IV. He has spoken to his staff, and he has been in contact with leaders of governments from around the world. And His Holiness recognizes the importance of dispatching himself. The Church comes before His Holiness. But this is something different. The pandemic has found a way to reappraise the situation.

As the social media numbers climb, more

accountabilities must be found. And yet, His Holiness remains resolute to listen to his heart and fulfill God's wishes absolutely. And God's freedom is suddenly on shaky ground, and human accountability appears like a good person to investigate.

The pandemic has put His Holiness in the spotlight, arguably more than any other time in history. His Holiness himself becomes a source of inquiry in terms of the pandemic. And yet, he has no stories to share. He is alone as much as anyone else against the tidal wave of mystery. For what it's worth, to see Marco searching for some answers is the kind of humble response that has awoken him this morning.

But there is also the sense that he has a responsibility. And suddenly, that burden is rather impressive, for His Holiness appears to question science. COVID-19 is undeniably a science problem, and His Holiness is aware of this as much as any layperson, but he still questions its reasoning. But for the Vatican, this is not a case of Catholicism against science, for that would be a silly debate to entertain given science's popularity in the world today. Rather, it is history that gives His Holiness's words the final say on the matter.

One of the scientists stands silently in the corner. He is from Chili and has no religious background whatsoever. He studied AI at Boston University and is dedicated to learning the relationship between human movements and technology. His Holiness once asked him how AI builds the essence of the soul? Ever since that little talk, some within the Academy feel he has sided with His Holiness rather than uphold the scientific promise and standard.

His Holiness leaves. Cardinal Peter grips the back of his chair and tries to compose himself. Suddenly, Marco senses the structure of authority. Cardinal Peter understands the process. Marco lowers his eyes. And it flutters inside the room as though it was bigger than any of its parts. But Marco also notices that Cardinal Peter is setting out plans to make sure the historical process is not lost on the Church. His Holiness will end up defeating this sick disease.

Marco and Hana arrive at the Boulder airport. There remains an unsettling buzz about the murderers. But they talk to each other, and he kisses her hair. She pulls at his shirt. Neither death, nor their pending separation, can dislodge their sense of love. Except, perhaps, an announcement from Air Rome.

It is something the Roman Catholic Church intends to control. It is a source reckoning for the Church. All the powers that be take notice of the disease, and suddenly its existence is much more real than before.

Cardinal Peter asks Marco to take the pictures off the wall.

"Put up a picture of His Holiness surrounded by children, for children are what represent strength during the pandemic. They are the ones that are the most tolerant towards the pandemic."

"Or else the elderly, or persons from Africa, as they are the most at risk to lose from the pandemic?"

"Why in heavens would you say that?"

"Facts, the things I hear on the news?"

"Never mind your feelings here, we are trying to create an image of His Holiness that is consistent with our times. We are not trying to be political or divisive."

"I see."

"Just choose something appropriate. And I don't care which continent the people come from!"

The conversation puts a smile on Marco's face. And he tries to show this feeling with Hirato, and also share that the events also appear slightly absurd.

Marco smiles at Hirato, who senses that something big is being discussed. Hana translates what has happened to her father, but Hirato takes no interest. Serena remains suspicious of Cardinal Peter. But he succeeds at ingratiating himself back into their lives. It turns out Cardinal Peter is not as squeaky clean as one might think. He visits prostitutes and drinks heavily. He just barely survives inside the Church. All of his days are spent in confession, trying to root out why he sins as much as he does. He tells Serena he is not any kind of guiding light for Marco. He is simply trying to help the boy out as much as he can. Serena finds his reasoning insulting, for she thinks that Marco deserves better.

"Don't take it personally. Just follow orders."

"That's all I ever do."

"That's all any of us ever do. So don't think you are special."

Hana has a different take on the situation. She thinks the Cardinal is acting differently to show him that it doesn't matter who comes to the office and visits.

Indeed, she thinks Cardinal Peter is trying to erase the fact that His Holiness has made an appearance. In other words, Cardinal Peter runs the office, and now that His Holiness has entered their space, they must change the decor to incinerate his memory as much as possible.

"But anytime His Holiness appears, it is a moment to celebrate."

"Well, only Cardinal Peter can answer those

questions."

Serena places the salad bowl on the table. She acts indifferent, but she can no longer resist. She squeezes Marco's shoulders, and gently asks what Hana has just said.

Now, she considers telling Marco all of the things she learned about Cardinal Peter, and to finally come clean. Because Hana is correct, and Cardinal Peter's actions are motivated out of self-interest.

Marco knows that his mother is taking on some swag that he has never seen before. She claims that she has sworn off men. She is merely putting things on pause while she decides how to go after some new fish and avoid any confrontations with Aldo.

Marco insists that is impossible. His mother does not have a pause button.

"I cannot believe my own existence does not clarify things for you ever?"

"What does that mean?" Serena is eager to have yet another discussion about the family, as she thinks it helps to steer Marco in the right direction.

"It means I don't know who my father is?"

"It could be lots of different men. I tend to think it is the one who was the lawyer from Romania."

"Mother?"

"Do you know how difficult it was to get you a birth certificate without your father's name?"

"No."

"Aldo needed to hire a very expensive lawyer. It was a big deal."

Marco shakes his head in disbelief.

And now he has trouble breathing, for whenever Marco's father is mentioned, he tends to feel anxious. Of course, Marco was only three when his dad was murdered in Paris, but his memory haunts him and his family to this day.

His memories of his father are rather vague. And his story is always changing given that Serena has been working with Milt, a screenwriter from Iowa, who has been conducting interviews with their family for over six years. His line of questioning has lurched into the disturbing.

They have kept this bit from Aldo to protect the writer, but Milt, Serena repeats in private, remains a fixture in their family.

Hirato wears Beats headphones, oblivious to the entire affair, and speaks to Midori about the possibility of coming home.

Hana cracks the window, a burst of wind flutters inside the spacious room. They have found a place of comfort, and they have no wish to leave.

"I deserve more from you."

"In what sense?"

"I just think we need to change so that we can start to feel more domestic. Because, as it stands, I feel like I'm always an outsider between you and your mother."

His Holiness holds a long face. And the solemnity works to distract Marco from his personal life and instead focus on the challenges of the Church. And now he wonders if His Holiness can sense his suffering. Marco's work ethic is acceptable, but to be recommended by Cardinal Peter, who lives a life of ruin inside the church, is no big compliment.

"You must realize by now the tremendous burden this puts on me."

"Of course, sir."

"And the number of deaths is increasing. It is a message from God, a reminder about man's fragility."

"Yes."

"But we must somehow focus on man's strength and recognize this is a great test for all of us. The way we react will show people the power of the Lord."

"But there are indications that we have power?"

"You must not think because there is no solution, and that you focus on that part of the pandemic, that you are somehow wise."

"No, I didn't say I was acting wise by making that point."

"We are here to serve God's needs. Think how much pain God feels right now?"

"I understand."

"You must realize that people are dying all around us, and it is a great sign of God's magnanimous nature. He is revealing to us the darkness of life and look how generous we are trying to help. Do you not understand?"

Revelation 21:4 says: "He will wipe away every tear from their eyes, and death shall be no more, neither shall there be mourning, nor crying, nor pain anymore, for the former things have passed away."

That God has forgiven the world of sin, and there will be no more death. And suddenly, instead of feeling God's grace, Marco is lost and estranged from the world. Marco needs to get His Holiness's attention, and see meaning in his life, the word of the Bible is too powerful to comprehend.

"They are the spirits of God's wakefulness. And we must be like them, and serve them, as God has shown them how to serve the world."

Marco stops at a little bar outside the Vatican. He rips open a pack of Camel Lights and drinks two pints.

Hana meets Marco when he arrives home. She is distraught as Hirato is unable to purchase a plane ticket to return home because of the pandemic.

"They have stopped my father from going home!"

"Pardon me?"

"Yes, my father cannot be with his parents, nor my mother. And he is slowly going insane living with you and your mother."

"Does he think we are too eccentric? Too Italian?"

"Never mind. He's just upset that now he is locked into living his final days in Roma. And he doesn't even like football."

Marco looks at the middle-aged woman who has just sat down. They entertain each other's attention. And then, in a sudden flash, he is overcome with guilt. He finds that he cannot stop objectifying her beauty. They continue to stare, and she appears relaxed at the characterization, as though she is used to this form of attention. Marco picks up his iPhone and tries to distract himself. She smokes very casually, almost inviting the obnoxious attention. Both men recognize each other well enough that they decide to explore this woman together. And what is it that Marco seeks? He repeats these things silently to himself, then detaches himself from her. Suddenly she is in pursuit of some self-respect.

Marco thinks he has been set up. He scratches the inside of his pant leg. He pays the bill. And now Marco somehow thinks that the waiter is part of the act. And no one can convince Marco otherwise. Not when this chump can be bought for a pack of Camels. And then he stops speaking Italian. He only drinks Caprini, from a dixie cup. And wears Clark's Wallabees.

She smashes the cigarette into the ashtray.

Next, she swaggers over to a man with a newspaper. She raises her hand and quickly smashes the paper down on the table. She holds a bridge over the table, like some poker champion posture.

Marco reflects on his faith. His Holiness's words are not guidance but orders. His Holiness works tirelessly to make Marco feel at home. And yet Marco remains swollen with fear about his job – the duties and execution of orders – and none of these things have made his understanding about being a Catholic any stronger.

The job ends as soon as American Airlines tells you it is safe to take off your seatbelt.

At that moment, when the stewardess practices a snarky stare, you can always lower your head and say a little prayer that you are far away from that place. You are safe. You might want to say "Amen".

Marco greets Martin, whom he has not seen for several months. Both men know so much has happened since the last time they saw each other. Indeed, Marco's entire life has changed, and his future is still unknown. Meanwhile, Martin remained in Japan, and has even begun practicing the language. He worked on a farm which sold cantaloupes for over one hundred American dollars. He was fired for eating cantaloupes on the job. His furious response was that only rich Americans were buying these cantaloupes, and how dare someone keep him stranded in that place.

The owner was not at all amused by his answer, and she replied, in broken English, that Martin was lucky that she had not called the police.

"I just happen to be in the neighborhood."

"I would say that is quite the coincidence!"

And they didn't say anything more about it even though it was a rather strange crossing of paths.

Martin eats a cannoli. He sips his cappuccino.

"I think it is totally interesting that you would come to Rome?"

"But I already told you I was travelling around the world."

The words hang in the air, and no one knows what to say. Marco takes it upon himself to try and act cool. Marco flings his arm into the air and asks the waiter to come over. He orders a bottle of San Pellegrino.

The two men begin to relax, and it is rather comforting that they would find the same sort of comfort they had found while in Japan.

"Do you mind if we continue our conversation?"

"What was that exactly?"

"Oh, you know, about Hiroshima."

"I don't know if we were ever talking about Hiroshima. I know that is where we met."

"But of course we were talking about it. Because you asked me about the politics of being an American, and how I felt about being in Hiroshima."

"I was just making friendly conversation. You don't have to think too much about it."

"I'm not. Not at all. But I could say the same about you, and the fact your country was part of the axis of evil."

"Am I required to reply to something like that?"

"I don't expect you have an answer, the same way as I don't have an answer about how my country settled matters."

They are in a state of shock at the same time. They make introductions as quickly and as easily as possible, and shower each other with compliments to try and put the other person at ease.

He smiles and then looks away trying to think of something to say. And Martin realizes that he has crossed the line. He was wrong to attack Marco because of what happened, but he must survive the conversation anyway.

The discomfort, or antagonism, is relayed around the room. One man, who wears a pinkish scarf and yellow glasses, is especially noticeable. He can tell that the men are not speaking properly to each other, but he can also see they are speaking English. Consequently, he makes no attempt to try and understand them. He takes the high road and feels rather proud that their conversation has somehow plummeted. Marco notices the conservative reproach, and gingerly looks back at Martin, and tries to communicate that everything is OK.

The waiter comes over to the table and asks if they want to order anything. But Marco is here to defend his friend, regardless of how they sound. He dismisses the waiter. And finally, he admits he likes the tension, the silence, the accusations, and especially the dangers about their conversation. This is the way war should always be talked about.

Martin exchanged emails with his ex-girlfriend, Anh, while he was in Japan. It happened rather unexpectedly, because he thought their relationship was over. But, one day, out of the blue, he received an email. It was one of those emails that included a birthday greeting, even though Martin's birthday was not until the middle of June, and it was only January.

Martin's first instinct was to trash the email, because that was what his psychologist, Benedictus, advised. Benedictus explained that there would be an underlying revenge scenario always brewing with Anh, and someday it was going to boil over.

Martin tried to explain to Benedictus that he had been through so much with Anh, and that breaking up was an impossibility. Their relationship was at full throttle. There might have been a separation, but they secretly remained a couple.

Benedictus reminded Martin of all the bad things that had occurred in his relationship with Anh, and that Martin's mental health could not take it anymore, as he would inevitably turn to drugs. But Martin explained that he didn't care about those things, and he still wanted to be with Anh.

Martin read the email with the utmost attention, and then he read it for a second and third time. So many things came to the surface. He was overly protective. He was clingy. He did not care about Anh's friends or family. As he looked over the list, it dawned on him that none of it was a true sign of someone who was in love. Anh was very much aware of Martin's treatment towards her and admitted that Martin had been like that since day one. And yet, for all those years, she let his rudeness slide. In fact, she found his rudeness endearing, because if she needed Martin to warm up to a particular person, she would give a little story about them, and soon Martin would be showering that person in compliments. The fact that Martin was never malicious towards her friends suggested that Martin was dependable and his gentle side could be relied upon. That was a tremendous breakthrough for Anh, and one she referenced constantly in their relationship.

Dear Martin,
I have thought about it for a very long time, and I have decided that I would like to get together again. I know that you have told me you want to split, but I cannot stand the idea of living apart from you. Life is not the same without you. Even when we fought, there was still a sense of comfort knowing that we were together. And now that we are apart, I find it hard to function.

Martin mulled over the email for some time. He ventured through Japan and found jobs at different farms. But he was never happy. He asked himself why he wasn't happy, and it dawned on him that, despite the fact that they fought constantly compounded with financial worries, he still had feelings for her.

Dear Anh,
My psychologist, Benedictus, has warned me that it is not good for my mental health to see you. But I decided to write to you anyway. I think of you constantly. But not in the way that you might think. I think of the different ways that you and I got in the way of each other's lives. I think of how much better things might have been if we had never met. Or else, I think of the time we wasted being with each other, when you could have been with some other nice young man. In other words, I am overwhelmed with memories of you, but not in the good sense. I understand that we might have shared time

together, but it would have been better served if you were with someone else. I am sorry to tell you this. You occupy a special place in my heart, but it is because I have regrets. It is because I think we could have done so much better if we had been apart. When you write to me and tell me that you miss me, I truly think you mean to say that we should never have met. That is the bond we share.

Ten minutes later, he received an email response: "I think you are right."

They were never meant to be. And yet, somehow, the American landscape made them fast friends and put them up to no good. The therapy helped, but it was his trip to the Far East that really showed him where they had gone wrong. If one wants to get really technical, it was the cantaloup farm, where Martin discovered that prize cantaloupes can sell for as much as one hundred dollars at the local market, and sometimes reach over a thousand overseas. They were a couple because society made them feel like they were meant to be together. Or else, he had a lazy attitude towards life, and Anh was a little withdrawn, and it was only natural that they should get together. He came up with many more theories which all suggested that America is succeeding at socialising the population into behaving, indeed dating, in such a way that suits America and not necessarily its citizens.

He travelled through Japan with a bag with an American flag patch on his shoulder. Whenever he was in big crowds, and he would notice someone gawking at the flag, he would take a second glance and try to see what they were looking at.

Next, his smile was an American smile, and how did the crowds react? The way he walked, his gait, his manner of checking the time, his facial expressions at finding out the cost of a meal. He reworked his entire personality in an attempt to disguise the signs by which people could tell where he was from.

This worked to merely filter out the types of persons who hate Americans for just being Americans. He did not learn anything about himself, only that there were types of people who simply chose to hate and would build on the mystiques of hate until they had lost all of their energy to say or do anything in that given situation.

Martin admitted that he had not learned anything about what it means to be an American.

He ventured forth into a new land, into Italy, to find the answers, and also to reconnect with Marco.

"I don't think this is a very productive conversation."

"I think it is quite obvious you don't like Americans."

"I don't think that question has ever come up. Have you thought perhaps you don't like Japanese, Italians, or Germans?"

Martin is momentarily speechless. He grabs the front of his tee, which is the concert tour tee for *Lose Yourself* by Eminem.

"I don't understand what you mean by that?"

"I'm curious if you have anything against any of those three countries?"

"But why would you put them together in that order?"

"Were they not the ones that you were once fighting against?"

There was another pause in the conversation.

"I think we have perhaps spoken enough about all of this. I did not intend to bring up the interplay between countries in the post-World War II."

"But is it not possible that you hold some resentment for the countries I mentioned?"

"I think that is only normal, the same way a black man does not love his country. The same way any country that was colonized has some resentment towards the colonial power."

"Oh, I think you are exaggerating. I think you Americans have anger issues towards the countries I mentioned."

"Perhaps that is true. But I find it curious that you would identify the problem in terms of us against you, when in fact you are quite blameless."

"I don't dispute that."

"I am not the most eloquent person. But I know that about myself. And the fact that you somehow still associate yourself with the divisions we've made in our conversation speaks against you."

"That we are somehow evil?"

"Yes."

"But I've never denied that. I've come to terms with that a very long time ago. Of course, we are evil. We are the evillest people the world has ever seen. And somehow Americans struggle with only the evil they have done, which you exhibit constantly, but you never want to admit is true."

"I am an evil person, Martin. Please try and understand that I feel quite the opposite when I think about you."

The woman comes directly over to Marco's table.

"I was wondering if you could lend me a couple of euro?" asked the mysterious woman.

"No…I haven't any money to spare."

The waiter wears his navy pants high, with an invisible, gray pinstripe. His shirt has a touch of yellow and the green bow tie is elegant. He has bulgy eyes, and it would be a shock to any of his customers to learn he had ever slept more than four hours at any one time.

With the choice to light a cigarette and include a light cough with a few gentle thuds on his chest, the waiter succeeds at opening the street to new ideas.

And for a moment, Marco realizes this is pure living. Marco squirms a little bit in his chair. He crosses his arms, and glances at the waiter one last time as he takes a long drag of his cigarette. He looks at the woman with the same eyes that invited her to sit down. And she is correct: he is being insincere. He has given her the wrong signals. Marco pokes his head up and looks at the woman and smiles. He scratches his head and motions for the waiter to come over.

"What did the young woman order?"

"An expresso."

"Let me get that for her."

The waiter goes inside the café. He returns with the change. The woman disappears (she looks over her shoulder one last time). Marco squares up towards his table, and she is invisible, and he fumbles with his iPhone and the newspaper. He acts fast, and thinks quicker, about the day that lies ahead.

"She probably pays three times out of ten. So don't feel bad."

"Oh, I don't feel bad. I like giving to charity too sometimes. Do you take me as some insensitive bastard?"

"Well, you don't look like someone who works with His Holiness. Let's put it that way."

They are fixed with murder. And all of their choices are drenched in blood.

And now the script from Boulder comes to an end. And it is only intermission. And trying to decipher what any of this means is impossible. Is this some message? Is this the murky world that surrounds death? The street hustle is always about death. It is not about helping someone. No one is offering Marco a second chance. They are fixated with death. With revenge. The Boulder crew are not interested in second chances. The outcome looks better with blood on their hands. Or else, a screaming lady. A man falls through a window. Someone is cut. Marco sighs at the depth of his imagination.

"These are the rules, and everyone has to get used to them."

"I agree."

"And besides, people are dying. Don't you think you deserve to drink a beer in peace, and not think that you are going to kill someone because droplets are coming out of your mouth?"

"I agree."

"Listen, I am just following the rules. We might not be able to stay open for much longer. So, everyone should just accept the rules."

"No question."

"And if this damn disease does eventually close my doors, I'm out of a job, and I'll be on the streets."

"Oh, I think they will get a handle on things long before something like that happens."

"Don't be so smart. And you know what gets me...? I'm used to complaining, and now I can't even say I'm going to move to the East Village in NYC and open a little place, because it is going to be the same thing there. This is madness."

The world is changing very quickly.

Cardinal Peter

Hana meets Marco on the street. She is crying. She rubs away her tears and stares into Marco's eyes until they are both overwhelmed with sadness.

"Cardinal Peter has died."

"What?"

"Last night. Suicide."

The words flutter in the air. And the game of death takes over. And Marco must come up with something. He pushes her away a little bit so he can look into her eyes. He rests his forehead on her shoulder and closes his eyes before turning and looking up into the sky.

He loosens their embrace, and his responsibility to Hana becomes his biggest concern. He tries to deny that Cardinal Peter ever existed. He thinks about Hana. Or else, her father, and the insecurities he feels living in Rome.

As he clenches his iPhone (his mother expects an answer) he is overcome with shame.

"I know, I know. I'm with Hana, and we'll be home shortly."

They sit on the curb, while Hana applies her make-up. And Marco acts like he is in deep contemplation. He ties his laces and fiddles through his wallet. He wipes his face free of tears. He rolls up the cuffs of his pants. They stand.

But he doesn't want to learn anything further. Or else, he doesn't know how to press play on their relationship. The streets are dangerous now. The drivers look unfriendly. One man notices Marco's gaze and gives him the finger. Hana smiles at the single mom and the fashionable baby carriage. The night weighs heavy, and honks, and joggers, and an English Bull Terrier on a long leash (they could get bit if they are not careful). Everyone is at each other's neck.

"Do you miss Japan?"

"Yes."

"But do you miss it more than being with me?"

"Not yet."

Serena stands in the kitchen and holds a glass of red wine. Hirato eats Stracciatella, a tasty egg soup, at the table. Diego stands in front of the TV and watches the football game.

The mother and son give a feeling of warmth about the place. And now Hana stands in the kitchen doorway, the atmosphere grows even more reflective.

"I didn't tell you he called me when you were away."

"I had no idea. And don't start telling me that you somehow caused him to kill himself. He had no right to do such a thing."

"He told me all sorts of things about his childhood. And his choice to enter the monastery. He was a good man because he was so separate from the rest of them."

"I thought he was a real curmudgeon."

"No, he was a gentle person, and he tried to make things right inside the Church. But how could he?"

"How could he?"

Marco stares at the TV, and silently cheers as Napoli scores a nice goal.

The dining room table becomes a destination where great generals meet to conquer the world. He presses his fingers on the schedule and checks for a home game within the next few days. The chaos of ordering football tickets prompts Marco to ask how Cardinal Peter died.

"He hung himself in the garden."

Hirato jumps in the air and begins to cheer.

"Wait, we can't cheer. That is not the right team?!"

"Goaaaaaaaaal!"

"We only cheer for A.S. Roma. We don't cheer for Spezia Calcio."

Hirato is the purest form of the fair-weather fan. He lifts his arms whenever a goal is scored.

By the start of the second half, Marco is already feeling a little drunk. But Hirato stands his ground.

The pandemonium of a goal is too much, and Hirato throws his sinewy arms into the air.

Marco stretches his arms upwards, half-way appeasing the situation, and then the two men get a good laugh out of their behaviour.

Marco looks at his iPhone, where he has a message from his mom.

"Cardinal Peter had no right to commit suicide. Especially since he was your boss. I find his conduct very cruel, and I'm sorry you must deal with this story. He would have known at an early age that the Church was not for him. And then to carry on: visiting prostitutes, drinking, and then killing himself. I have no sympathy for him. He could have left a vacancy for someone else. But nooo, he decides to live the lie. The Church is full of skilled bastards."

"Take a breather, Rocky."

Hirato is slumped over and snores. A touch of nervous energy comes over Marco, as he didn't spend a fortune for someone to fall asleep at the game. A frantic goal by Roma, and immediately both men are on their feet again, cheering the home team.

Marco suggests they leave and beat the crowds.

A group of police officers rushes towards the exits. Hirato grabs Marco's arm and asks what's going on. A man stands near the bar and brandishes a gun, awkwardly changing positions, pointing it at the police officers. Marco makes eye contact with the man, and suddenly all semblance of individual freedom disappears.

The police decide how things are going to end.

The crowds scream as the police smother the man. Hirato refuses to let go of Marco's arm. The man is hidden. And now the police begin to filter through the crowds. Marco and Hirato are perplexed, and how strange they feel, because they are no longer interested in the medley, but rather the quick exit.

They manage to escape onto the Rome Metro. And right when the doors close, there is a hard smack on the outside of the window, and the face of Gil appears, a heavy from Boulder, who is hired to make sure the job runs smoothly.

Marco does not venture too distant in his imagination, nor does Hirato, for they have both shared something powerful earlier. Instead, Marco looks at the destination display, choreographing their next move.

His feet dangle off the side of the bed. Hana scampers around the room. She holds a short, black, Chanel dress, and drapes it over Marco's knee.

Marco can hear his mother in the kitchen.

"Do you like Chanel?"

"Yes, of course."

"I like some of their stuff."

Marco smiles and turns towards the closed door.

"Thank you for taking my dad to the soccer game tonight."

"It was the least I could do, given that he is imprisoned in Italy."

"He appreciates everything that you've done for him. And he intends to pay you back someday."

"I don't understand what you mean?"

"Japanese men are very proud. But they are also very emotional. And he sees that you are trying to help, which in turn means he will try and help you someday."

Hirato recalls his time as a young man growing up on the tough streets of Tokyo: My background is quite different from others who have become Yakuza. There are some who are born into the life, but most find their way after a brilliant early career in crime. And then I got an invitation to join. My life suddenly changed overnight. I used to love riding my Suzuki at breakneck speeds. And all the bars full of beautiful women. And we were respected in all of the bars. I was a hired buckaroo. I was immune to violence. My voice was stiff and calculating. And I made money. I was feared. Chefs would pass out while making me a steak. Midori loves that I became a vegetarian because the chefs were all dead. Dead, dead, dead!

Cardinal Stewart is from Dublin, where he has worked as a parish priest for the past twenty or so years. Cardinal Stewart pinches the bottom of his crucifix and raises it slightly in front of him and whispers that they must pray. Cardinal Stewart holds out his hand and waits for Marco to touch his hand before he speaks.

"Let us pray for Cardinal Peter. He was a kind spirit…"

"Amen to that!"

"His Holiness wants to meet with you later today."

"I usually meet with him on Mondays anyway, to discuss the latest Twitter numbers."

"Yes, of course. But he wants to discuss your relationship with Cardinal Peter."

"Of course."

Cardinal Stewart is displaying an abundance of knowledge about his role even though he has just taken the job.

"His Holiness knows that you were very close to Cardinal Peter, and he just wants to speak to you about a few things. His Holiness will also be hosting a private ceremony for Cardinal Peter, and he wishes for you to attend."

"Of course."

"I think it is imperative that you attend."

"Yes, of course. I've known Cardinal Peter for so long, I will be attending without question."

"He was troubled. I had even begun to pray for him recently. I could tell there was something amiss. However, I would never have predicted he would have taken his life. I was mostly praying for him to stop smoking."

"His Holiness told me the same thing."

"Yes, well, we always thought he needed to quit smoking. And I always found it rather odd that he would share that his doctor never found anything wrong with him. But I digress, I prayed a lot for him. I used to smoke. I told him so. And I got the patch, and it worked immediately. God had nothing to do with it. The patch saved my life. But he didn't want any of it."

Marco checks his jacket to make sure his cigarettes are not showing. Cardinal Stewart releases Marco's hand and leaves. The room is heavy, darker, and, despite failing to live a good Catholic life, the world is suddenly awkward, serious, and lacks humour.

He stares out the window. The crowds of tourists. Some of them are guilty. And suddenly the cardinal's life is in dispute. There is no reason for a suicide, but there are lots of reasons for a murder.

"Perhaps His Holiness knows the truth. How did he die?"

"He can do as he pleases. He has an epiphany... he can begin to exercise his faith for the Lord in ways he never imagined. No one will be watching."

Cardinal Stewart appears in the doorway. A quivering smile. They have finally broken the ice.

It will happen from time to time where you don't know what to say, and you may feel a little lost. The job has caused you to act in an extraordinary way. Naturally, run ins are to be expected.

Marco's mind begins to race, and now he sees his life flash before his eyes, like Cardinal Peter smoking at the front entrance of the Vatican, or else down the street, a couple of members of the Delaware crew plotting their next crime binge.

"Excuse me!"

"Pardon me. Aldo, son, and you..."

And then together, as though magically, they say:

"Peace comes over those..."

"I don't want you to feel any undue pressure on the job. For example, someone will eventually be coming in to help you. But you must understand these things take time. Perhaps you could just continue your daily routine as you would before. Just imagine if Cardinal Peter was still alive."

Suddenly, his thoughts about Cardinal Peter are confused. He should have been thinking about how to maintain a sense of order. Or how to cherish his memory. Maybe even make notes of some of his teachings.

His Holiness inspects the Twitter feeds, printed on glossy paper, which lie on the table.

"Peace comes over those who seek comfort from the Lord."

"I have not yet posted that comment, but it is one that I like very much."

"OK, I will note that."

"But there are so many quotations we can use. Or else you can post something you prefer."

His Holiness waits until Marco finishes before they speak. And then His Holiness raises his eyes, and looks at Marco, and explains that Cardinal Peter is in heaven, but his tenure made his journey a little topsy-turvy.

The Church is indifferent about its own people. Moreover, as Marco reflects, it would take a fleet of conspirators to make a murder happen at the Vatican.

His Holiness is not the one to hear Marco's confession. Cardinal Peter died a normal death – by his own hands. Not knowing the truth is torturous.

And suddenly Marco is overcome with guilt and remorse. Finally, he sees himself in Cardinal Peter's world. He could have asked a question, volunteered to do something with him. A simple act of kindness. But Marco never tried any of these things. Instead, Marco remained steadfast in his role: Cardinal Peter was hard-nosed, and one should never cross his word. Had he taken the opposite approach, maybe Cardinal Peter would be alive today.

His Holiness holds a wry smile, the saintly face disappears. The office feels different. The birds swoop in ways that exhibit a greater knowledge about their lives.

A slew of cardinals enters the room. His Holiness focusses a long stare at Marco, showing everyone they have not finished speaking. Everyone fades towards the perimeter of the room.

His Holiness returns to the prints of the Twitter feeds. He looks over the prints and nods accordingly. He looks very pleased and wants to congratulate Marco.

"They all look perfectly good to me."

"Yes."

"The numbers. They look like they are improving also. Although not as high as Katy Perry."

"You always mention her?"

"She holds the golden egg when it comes to Twitter and Instagram."

"Yeah. We'll get there." Marco flashes a rare smile at His Holiness.

The name-dropping session is not some arbitrary slip of the tongue. It is Pope Faustino showing Marco the breadth of his reach. It has nothing to do with Katy Perry, but the name resonates with a very large fan base. And the Church pursues any kind of fan base it can get its hands on.

From the far reaches of the hallway, the room appears like a great destination.

His Holiness greets the invitees. And now Marco looks around and feels a little intimidated. Marco lightly taps his pen on the medieval table and looks at His Holiness.

"I think you are right. We live in difficult times."

"And that is something we must learn to discuss."

"Yes, I think you're right. Let's start addressing the importance of science in the world today!"

"Very good, Your Holiness."

"You said it correctly."

"Pardon me?"

"I always told Cardinal Peter that you should address me as 'Your Holiness'. Not because I don't like to be called something different, but you always appeared more comfortable saying it like that whenever you mentioned my name that way."

The Academy of Science is composed of lifetime members that are appointed by His Holiness. The purpose of the Academy is to provide His Holiness with the most up to date science on questions that impact the Church.

Since COVID-19, the Academy tries to meet with His Holiness at least once per day. And the weight of these meetings puts tremendous pressure on His Holiness.

For as much as pure science rules their findings, His Holiness has another idea, namely, to seek out God's plan behind the numbers.

Cardinal Peter continues to be the focus of all their conversations. Serena is obsessed with why someone as smart as Cardinal Peter would enter the monastery, when he knew full well he was not made for the Church.

Matthew 5:28 says: "Anyone who looks at a woman lustfully has already committed adultery with her in his heart."

They are being followed. And they are the same ones behind the cardinal's death. And Serena, who knows all of Marco's games, no longer trusts Hana. That is what keeps the young couple up at night. They could be next.

Each night, Marco retells the conversation he had with his mother to Hana. The torture of these sessions is compounded by the fact that Hana already has a good sense of what they were saying. The irony, of course, is not knowing what happened to Cardinal Peter, and what information Serena has about his death.

"I once considered another life when I was much younger. My mother and father warned me about the kind of life that was expected given the pressures of different people around us. And I remain grateful to them for that. Yet, there remains an evil path, and I choose to follow it. And it is very well paved and offers endless possibilities. And I intend to make it darker. And I shall turn beautiful as I explore this path. And I shall someday show my children the path I have chosen. Do you understand? I am grateful for all I have been provided. And you can't make me think otherwise," reflected Hana.

Midori insists that Hana should find out more about Cardinal Peter.

And yet Hana has already shared as much as she can. And the sense of not knowing how he died creates an intolerable feeling of sabotage. What's more, the fact he might have been murdered puts an even greater strain on Cardinal Peter's memory.

"Mother, I need to discuss something with you."

"It will have to wait. I have an important meeting."

"We must discuss Cardinal Peter."

"We talked about him over supper last night, what

more do you want to say?"

"We need to stop talking about him immediately. His memory is driving me insane."

"I have to meet Giorgio's sister."

"What?"

Marco begins to eat his breakfast: some leftover lasagne from the night before and a fried egg.

And the phone rings, and there is no one there.

"Yes, she called me last night. And wants to meet."

"What on earth are you going to discuss with her?"

"That is what the meeting is about. I am rather confused myself."

Serena had agreed to meet Giorgio's sister Bianca at a bistro. Serena arrives a little early and orders a Negroni. She is wary, for she is being stared at by a seductive man at a table in the dining area. The bartender assumes an easy place to look at him, for he is acting shifty and purposeful. Also, there is his soft bronze glow, or the wrinkly neck, face, and forehead. Finally, she is undone by the bartender's silky blue tie. He acts nervous at the peering, heavy eyes, and when he pushes the glass forward on the mahogany bar, he glances at Serena, and next shifts his eyes towards the affluent, elderly man. She is being insulted in the most sophisticated way possible. And her only defenses are more drinks and rattling off how easy it is to screw an old man for money.

She peers at the wood-paneled ceiling: at the indirect light, the peachy glow.

"I assume you are Serena?"

"Yes, Bianca?"

"Giorgio only liked big-chested girls."

Serena dances her fingers in front of her face, a touch

embarrassed by the comment.

"There was a man inside the bar, and he was making me feel very uncomfortable, and I decided to go outside."

"I hope Giorgio never made you feel like that..."

They can peer around the bar and not feel intimidated anymore. They can laugh at their sense of power. The rich, old man looks like a grizzly, old mafia boss, who has lost all zest for life. Perhaps, if he was younger, he could take on the two ladies, with charm and influence. Instead, he is a target for gossip and innuendo. Or old-time mafia stories, which the ladies fall for, but when the stories run dry, they are more interested in speaking softly to each other about their own pasts. He puts his drink down and slumbers through his own personal journeys, which are enough to keep him alert enough to order another drink and forget his surroundings.

Serena learns that Giorgio was married. And he has several children who live in Milan. Giorgio had no contact with his children, but Bianca tries to keep up with them as much as possible. She has not missed a birthday or Christmas since they were little. He was eventually arrested for an assault. Apparently, he was found sleeping on the street, and then decided to jump on the back of a street-cleaner and try to remove the driver from the truck. He drove the truck into a ditch, which required several top-ranked engineers and a crane to remove the truck from the side of the road.

Serena covers her face as she laughs. She can picture Giorgio running up the street, scaring the daylights out of the driver.

She is curious about the children, whether or not they require any support. Bianca answers all of her questions a little matter-of-factly. She senses there is an ulterior motive. But rather than put too fine a point on it, Serena orders another round of drinks.

"I just think there might be some chance that his death didn't need to happen?"

"Well, we are all going to die someday."

"Yeah, and Giorgio was not the best person in the world, but I still don't think he deserved to die. Do you have any ideas how he might have died?"

"I thought the coroner said he hit his head after a long night of drinking?"

"Yeah, but that sounds a bit odd."

Serena looks at the man at the bar. By now he is drunk, and he refuses Serena's attention. And then her iPhone rings, and she notices it is Marco.

She turns the iPhone to silent mode.

"It is just a theory. I don't know if it is true. But it is something that has crossed my mind. And I have a responsibility to his kids, to get the right answers."

"I still don't know what you are trying to say. I feel a lot of pressure right now. I wish you would just stop."

They are no longer talking as girlfriends. Bianca is interrogating Serena, to find out how Giorgio really died. And because Serena pursues the same line of questioning, she does not resist being a temporary target. Indeed, she wants the conversation to accelerate, she has never felt so close to someone in her whole life.

"Girl, do you want another drink?"

"Yes."

They order Bellini cocktails. Their glasses clink. Serena holds her drink a moment longer, and Bianca recognizes their bond and gives a little fist pump and wink.

Serena promises herself she will never rat on Aldo, and Bianca is strong enough to deal with all the obnoxious lies. They need more drinks and more years of living before they will ever feel like they dealt with the situation as best they could. And right now, they miss Giorgio terribly.

His binge drinking has become very serious indeed. Hana tries to help her father into bed. His habit is manageable. But his general attitude has changed.

The calls to her mom are non-stop: he mopes around, he has stopped eating, and he forgets to flush the toilet. He wants the attention. Or else, he acts out so he can assess how his behaviour is affecting other people around him.

Midori knows her husband too well, and these kinds of behaviours are him acting out because he is away from home. These are not signals of a broken man. Far from it. But Hirato does not have the resources to tell this to her daughter.

Hirato receives a call in the middle of the night. Naomi is having difficulty breathing. She thinks the feeling will go away.

Naomi is taken to the hospital. When the paramedics arrive, they wear full suits and masks, or PPE. The paramedics are gentle, but as Naomi tries to ask questions, no one answers.

She lies in the back of the ambulance. She rolls her eyes upward, evading contact with the foggy oxygen mask. The sirens, and now she imagines the flickering lights, and the hulking bodies getting comfy for the drive to the hospital, and she dreads this is the last thing she will see before she dies.

Naomi is taken to the fourth floor, where she is placed in the hallway with a number of patients. They cannot defend themselves. They are by-products of the pandemic. They cannot raise their hands and demand for the ombudsman to take care of things. They are invisible, for no one wants to see this side of the pandemic. And the pandemic conveniently hides them from everyone, because the disease must show its reach as something brutal and deadly. And after the long hours of waiting, even the wall of patients, who are a source of freedom to each other, begin to suspect each other – part of the pandemic's wrath, and they curl into their own minds, and suddenly feel alone again.

Naomi is placed inside a room with three other patients. All of the patients act like they are friends. And they contemplate death. An elderly man in his eighties accepts that he has lived a good life.

A middle-aged woman instructs her husband about a recipe for black sesame cookies, the names of their kids' teachers, and to send birthday cards to all of their nieces and nephews.

Breathing becomes Naomi's primary focus. She starts to cough and twists and turns in her bed. The nurse, Shawni, is kind, and stays by her side. But she is overworked and says things to Naomi that do not make sense. At one point, Naomi wrenches her arm away from the nurse and calls Midori.

"What the hell are you doing? I tried calling you?!"

"The hospital is crazy. Even the nurse who is supposed to provide motivation and support seems a little off. She kept repeating to me that my husband would be arriving soon."

"That's odd?"

"I don't think I am going to make it."

"Are you able to drink something? Maybe have some chocolate, or something?"

"I am about to die!"

"Stop it."

Naomi begins to cough. She smiles at Shawni beside her and raises her iPhone into the air.

"I'll call you back."

Naomi is her mom's best friend. And Naomi is a saint. And Naomi sacrificed her whole life to help her little sister become successful. And she has no regrets about helping her little sister.

Hirato locks himself in the guest bedroom. Two days later, he opens the door, whereupon Hana runs inside and hugs her father. Serena stands in the doorway. Hirato begins to cry out of frustration. Hana tries to hold her father, but he turns combative.

Despite the importance to mourn Naomi's death, there is an even stronger feeling to try and lift Hirato's spirits.

At first, he takes a few steps into the hallway, sliding his hand against the wall, and speaks some gibberish. He establishes a routine when he starts to take breakfast, lunch, and supper. Hana tries to talk to her father during this time, but he merely raises an eyebrow and continues with whatever task he is doing. As strange as it sounds, Serena finds she is growing closer to Hirato during this time. Perhaps it is just because they have stopped trying to communicate. She recognizes all his different actions. Or else, she is privy to the news in Japan through Hana, and that Hirato has cut himself off from learning any more news. She feels she has knowledge that she could share with Hirato, if they began to talk again. Or else, quite possibly, Serena has just finished mourning the death of Giorgio, and she recognizes the signs of sadness that Hirato displays.

Serena underestimates Hirato's state of mind. He is, in fact, caught up in an existential crisis. And Hana feels very humble in front of her father during this time, because she recognizes he is going through something he should never have experienced. In other words, Hirato suffers so much being away from home, it is a miracle he is still alive. She prays he will not kill himself, because if she were him, she probably would have done so many weeks ago.

Hirato starts to come back to life. When he speaks, he offers a smile. They are random, and his attitude, generally speaking, has not improved. Indeed, the moments of lucidity are a sign of a much bigger problem. It is clear, however, that he wants to speak and get better.

Hirato taps his finger on the passenger window.

"He likes the tall buildings. That's all."

"Tell him we can drive past them some more, if you want?"

"Yes, he wants you to stop the car, so he can look at the tall buildings."

Marco parks the car. Hana takes a picture of Hirato at the side of the car. Hirato becomes disorientated and wants to go back to the car. Marco looks at Hana for an explanation.

"He wants to sit in your car."

"Why?"

"Because he needs to rest."

He holds her in his arms. He grips her shoulders, and watches as Hana's eyes fill with tears.

The conference room door is open slightly, and Hana

decides to enter. She looks at the peach ceiling and sprawling light fixtures. One thick-bearded man and his partner sit close to each other and eat cereal. Suddenly, American landmarks flash in her mind like the Gateway Arch, Mount Rushmore, and the Statue of Liberty. She has come great distances for unspeakable reasons.

Midori shares the conversation with the others, and it turns out that Hirato has no memory of the last couple of weeks.

Marco grips his waist, and then, with the other hand, reaches down and pinches his pant leg near the thigh, and lightly yanks it up. He has a flashback of the time when his doctor told him he had an irregular heartbeat.

Hana appears a little confused, but then she notices the counterman waving, and then quickly walks to the back of the room, pulling the duffle bag full of money.

Hana cannot take her eyes off Marco.

The only evidence of the job is the one you carry in your head. The thumping heart, the racing heart, the ticker that starts to overboil. That slab of meat that somehow knows everything. And if we could get rid of everyone's hearts, we would do that too.

"But we must plan our trip to China, where we will be safe."

"I don't want to live in China."

"OK. Then I'll come home. We can decide later how we will live our life."

Marco orders a bottle of champagne.

If the champagne works to change the atmosphere, all will be a success. They will have found a space to be a family. And as they drink, it dawns on Marco, and everyone else for that matter, they are feeding the mythology as they go along. They feel livelier.

Hirato grabs his flute of champagne and raises it into the air. He breaks into a speech, which instantly brings Hana to tears. He discusses the pandemic in China, and the world's slow response, and how innocent people are dying unnecessarily. How Naomi has been taken away from them, dying unnecessarily. She is the closest thing to a saint as they come. Only pure evil could have caused her death.

Suddenly, everyone recognizes the burden to speak about this episode. There is unanimous resolve to leave this place and reconvene in a few weeks from now.

Instantly, priest, congregation, and society share a moment of calm, at the impossibility to speak God's words.

They stumble back to the car. Hirato looks up at the skyscraper that spires into the sky. He smiles and looks at Marco and Hana.

Aldo loves his wife because she is at his side when he goes to bed each night. He meets other women regularly at sleezy motels, creepy bars, or the basement laundry rooms of nondescript buildings. And these women know that Aldo is a family man. Indeed, for several years now, he has been mostly partaking in the sex precisely because he thinks it is good for business. Most of the women he meets are Chatty Cathies, and it will get around that Aldo is making the rounds. Invariably, Aldo will get a call the next day from one of his mobster friends, and the business cycle will repeat itself over and over.

But running a mix of legit and illegal companies while supporting Serena and providing guidance to Marco is not as simple as it sounds.

In truth, he has enough common sense to know that his secretive side is essentially a bad person. He treats this part of his personality as though he has a drug problem. And the seedy world he visits is the effect of using. And you can imagine how intimidating it feels given how recklessly he is living. Indeed, his monthly budget alone (the cost of the mortgage, wife and kids, and Serena and her family, plus the overheads at his legitimate companies, and then all the illegal activities), would shock most people to pieces. But Aldo is fastidious and seems to be handling everything OK. He lies in his bed and looks over at Tina: he is filling out a tax ledger, and as long as Tina is beside him each night, he knows he is doing OK. Once the money stops, Tina will be gone in a heartbeat. Lately, however, it is not just money. One day, at breakfast, Tina blurts out that she doesn't know her husband anymore. She couldn't care less who she sleeps with. She admits she might notice little improvements, whether or not her partner can last more than one minute, but besides that she does not have many other expectations.

Aldo recalls the time when he was building his career as a mobster: I needed to prove myself on every job back then. Try getting out of a private plane at LaGuardia Airport in the middle of the night, in the middle of the winter. You know, just being from Italy has its problems, and the payoffs were killing me.

From the neighbors to the hire-a-cop; from the electricians to the 7-Eleven clerks, and then the logistics of finding a safe house. Jobs were a full-time racket back then.

Today is a little bit different. Once I'm committed to do a job, and it doesn't happen all that frequently anymore, but when it does, I'm already in the safe house counting the loot. There is no fear, no more sweats, I haven't clipped someone in five years. Forget about it!

Aldo was very close to his father. Indeed, Sylvester was very honest with his son about their lifestyle and made no attempts at hiding their background. The truth of the matter is Sylvester was never a big-time player. He was never a high roller in the mafia game. He was a mid-level enforcer but spent most of his working life as a dispatcher for a trucking company. Whenever money got tight, he would set up a job. He would set up one of his own trucks to get jacked, and it was always a new driver. But that happened very infrequently. The insurance companies started to catch on.

Aldo and Serena grew up in a working-class family for the most part. But because the mob was always a part of their lives, there was always the feeling that they could do better. Of course, Serena didn't want any part of the business. She had friends whose families had been killed. Or else, she hated all the news she read in the newspapers. Or else, she disliked the reputation of the mafia in popular culture and the movies. But Aldo was different. He couldn't get enough of it. And just being on the fringes was enough for him to almost go insane. And so, with the lively stories of his father, or else whenever he visited his father at work, seeing cargo being unloaded and reloaded, he became fascinated with the business model.

Sylvester always knew about other crews trying to get wise on a shipment. Sylvester would come home and put his delivery papers in a safe each night. A shipment of sardines was big money for a small-time hood who could let go of the loot for a quarter of its retail worth and still make a small fortune. Aldo learned really quickly that it was never the bad guys you had to worry about, it was the crumbs, the street trash, who were clinging to life and who needed a break that you had to watch out for.

Everyone in the neighborhood knew that Sylvester was someone who could make someone rich.

And then, one day, Aldo admitted he could not sit around and feel stressed about his father anymore. He took it upon himself to become a made guy. If someone wanted to mess with Sylvester, they would have to mess with Aldo first.

But choosing to be a tough guy had consequences, given the blurry connection Sylvester had with the mob. In other words, everything that Aldo did was watched under a microscope.

One night, for example, Aldo attended a party, and he decided to fight the owner of the house. The owner was in his fifties and considered a rather important person in the illegal fish trade. Aldo beat the man silly. These kinds of impromptu beatings continued for quite some time. Before long, he had the reputation of a tough guy. But he had also earned the reputation of beating the shit out of men who are in their forties and fifties. He acquired a rather comedic reaction from most people. And then, one time, while on vacation in the South of France, he went to a night club and got into a fight and killed someone.

He was immediately arrested. His time in prison secured his reputation. He earned a level of respect that most people never see in their entire lives. Indeed, it was the type of respect that most people try and avoid.

After a short stint in prison, and the suspended

sentence offered to people who are connected, he returned home. Sylvester was the first to greet his son and immediately told him how proud he was of the man he had become.

These are not the kinds of conversations that will make it into a Shakespearean play. These are talks between a downtrodden, older man and his ambitious, angry son, who had no resources save the lofty ideas of becoming a gangster and doing everything in his power to achieve his goal.

Serena, meanwhile, began to push away from her family. Whenever Serena tried to speak to her mother and ask that she change the situation, she was always ignored. Ultimately, she was told she must love her brother because he was trying to make the family better.

Aldo caused a rupture in the family. He was the one who decided to go beyond the tolerable behaviour of his father and attract more and more attention to the family. Meanwhile, Serena's mother, Martina, remained indifferent, and pretended nothing had changed. By the time Aldo was seventeen, he was already pulling in a lot of money from his different business ventures. For example, he lifted a truck full of DVDs, and soon had one of Europe's finest DVD collections. He opened little shops around Rome and was making money hand over fist. He discovered the value of being an event planner.

And then he discovered fast food joints, which are hugely profitable, and he could off-load goods out the back door.

An audacious police captain, with a few nights of surveillance, destroyed Aldo's plan in a snap.

Around that time, Serena started to date Frank, who was a member of a famous crew from Sicily. Serena had no interest in marrying a mobster; however, Frank was slick and smitten with Serena, and he denied he was a made guy. They started a family. Meanwhile, Aldo was still living at home and becoming increasingly resentful towards his sister for marrying a made guy.

Serena liked that Frank worked part-time at the local garage. He lived at home until he was close to thirty. He ate with his family each night and presented a very normal lifestyle to the outside world.

It turned out, Frank was a jewellery expert. He organized heists all around the world. He could discuss special gems with museum precision. He was consulted for his expertise. And he participated in the occasional jewel heist. All during this time, he never mentioned anything to Serena.

It remained a secret until that fateful day when Serena opened the *Roma Times* and saw a picture of Frank in a puddle of blood in the Diamond District in Paris, in the first arrondissement.

Aldo took the death of Frank harder than Serena, for he had always thought that they were going to become business partners one day.

Aldo interrupts Tina before she can finish and explains that he has always provided for his family. And they should expect nothing more. Besides, he says, speaking and endeavoring to know every secret about the other person is overrated: "we drive a Mercedes Benz. That should be enough."

Tina gets dressed and prepares for the day. Aldo clears his plate, which includes a half-eaten crostata, or jam tart, and goes upstairs. Tina remains at the table and continues to eat cannellini bean stew with egg, a popular morning meal from the Tuscan region. Tina has put the kids in the backseat of the car, when she finds Aldo blocking the driveway.

"You're not going out today."

"Get out of the way."

"I'm taking you and the kids on a drive."

"Both of them have a test today."

"Is that true? Too bad. We're all going for a drive!"

The children are unconscious. So is Aldo. Tina has difficulty breathing. She is able to scream enough to trigger the paramedics to come around to the passenger door.

She cannot detach the terror of the moment, and then she lets down her guard, and opens her heart to the sliver of a chance that the others are alive.

They use metal cutters to remove the roof. Aldo is in the fetal position on the floor. Tina is caught between the passenger seat and the passenger door. They are placed on stretchers and rushed to the hospital. The crash is reported widely by all the news stations.

Dante and Izmania each have matching broken legs. Tina has numerous broken limbs, including both femurs, and both arms. Her lower teeth are shattered. The brake stick went through Aldo's mouth and out the back of his neck. His leg has a three-part compound fracture. A doctor flies in from Turkey and another one from Paris. Aldo is in surgery for four days.

Two months later, the family are together inside Aldo's hospital room and eat Chinese take-out. And Aldo, who lacks manners, asks Tina if she wants to repeat to everyone that he is not a dead fuck.

"I was exaggerating. It is closer to five minutes."

"That's better."

Aldo recognizes he has taken on too much responsibility. Upon his announcement, he is faced with more people staring at him, and now he wonders what harm he has brought upon them.

Truth be told, Aldo is rather bored by the reaction. He feels outraged that the others cannot see the claws of death and he cannot stop being who he is. The best he can do is deflect the anger from everyone at the table. This tends to make everyone think the good life is still within reach. This reaction tends to incense Aldo even more and further dilutes any justification to change his life.

A young doctor enters the room and puts his hand on Aldo's shoulder.

Aldo feels safe around his doctor. Aldo tries to bring the doctor closer to his family.

"This is my sister."

"Your brother has a strong constitution."

"She is going to live with me and take care of me."

"I think that sounds terrific. But based on how well you did in surgery, I bet you'll be back on your feet in no time."

"Right, Serena?"

"I've got a place."

"We're going to sell it. OK, Serena?"

"OK, Aldo. If that's what you want?!"

Serena lies on the couch, unable to sleep. She brings the covers up to her chest. She looks around the room. Marco and Hana talk quietly in the bedroom.

Back in Boulder, it is early morning, and the hotel looks ordinary conducting its daily routine. Some cleaning staff huddle by a side door, jabbering with the food delivery truck driver, covering all the main bases: immigration, health care, education, and especially the Broncos.

Inside the conference room, the light switch pushes against the heel of Hana's palm. And then, she turns the lights on and off several times.

She approaches the counter and then reaches down and grabs the Glock that is attached to her ankle. She points her gun at the counter, and then peers over at Marco.

The snarky hotel owner from Mumbai can't take it anymore. He smashes his fork down, pushing his crown rib with the inside of his inexpensive suit. He rises to his feet and parks both hands against the side of the table, like he is a snooker player plotting his next shot.

"What the fuck kind of meeting is this? And she has the guts to show up late? Her father messed us up back in the day. And you continue to make me wait?"

Marco removes his gun and scans the room. Hana nods at Marco. She goes over to the door and politely waits.

They will sell the apartment. Marco will go out on his own. And she will leave the neighborhood. A chance to change her life. Suddenly, all the steps she needs to take are simple ones.

There is an all-night gas station not far from the apartment. She buys some eggs and a loaf of bread. She does not recognize the clerk. Aldo has planted it in her mind that she was never from this place. She is finally returning home.

The clerk speaks to her as if they know each other.

"Just this please. I don't have very much time."

"That's OK. I understand. I was just trying to be friendly." The clerk is embarrassed with the interaction.

Serena taps her hands on the counter.

"I'm sorry. I didn't hear what you said, and that is why I reacted the way I did."

"OK, I…"

"I had no right to be like that."

She pours OJ into a glass, and then finally begins to make coffee. Marco appears. He stares at the table and sits down.

"I have an announcement to make."

"I assumed so, but I was not sure…"

"I saw your uncle yesterday. And we talked. And he's invited me to move in with him."

Marco goes over to the sink and peers outside. He turns to his mother and smiles.

Marco sits in the airplane and peers over towards the terminal, but Hana is no longer there. She has returned to her gate to return home to Tokyo. "Will I be returning to this place?" he asks himself.

A tall, thin man with his hair slicked back sits down next to Marco. They make introductions without saying hello, just a long steady handshake which helps the man get comfortable.

In mid-air, the man beside Marco curls his copy of *Sports Illustrated* and tucks it into the seat pocket in front of him. He dances his fingers on his lap, and then turns abruptly to Marco, and gives the impression he will never leave.

"Yes?"

"Couldn't miss you two."

And I'm bored, Marco reflects. I've played this part my whole life. They stand around me and can't speak. And demand, demand, when truthfully, I know all of their thoughts before they think them. It is the one job I never wanted.

Serena rises to get Marco's attention to watch the football game.

Hirato appears a little lost. Marco points towards the kitchen, where his breakfast is sitting on the kitchen table.

"Your uncle has provided us with so many opportunities already. And now I must repay him, by helping. And besides, I don't have any other obligations."

"Keep us busy?"

"Yes, he nearly died."

"Yes, and I think it would have been much better had he just died instead of what you are about to do."

"What does that mean?"

"He is trying to control you. He knows that he is vulnerable, and he'll no longer be able to come over here."

"That is not true."

"At least you have some independence living here. Even though he pays for everything."

"I'll have my own room, a separate entrance."

Hirato mentions that there is tension in the apartment. And then Midori, who thinks she has a good sense of timing, and a big fan of *We Love Raymond*, says: "there will always be tension, they are Italian!"

"He's been in his room all day."

"And do you think that sounds normal?"

"Oh, he had some visitors."

"Visitors?"

"Cousins. They came to visit for a little bit."

Marco had to step back for a moment. Suddenly, the scene feels different. And yet Marco feels it is unfair to ask any follow-up questions.

"Who were your cousins again?"

"Huh? My dad's brother's kids. His son."

"Oh, right, of course."

And they both feel they are in a lie. And now, Marco is paralyzed with fear. He is suddenly puzzled by his feelings and the situation. He feels a little bit of sweat at the back of his head.

"Where are your cousins now?"

"They've already left."

Marco wants to ask more questions, but something makes him stop. He is thinking about tomorrow. He smiles gently at Hana, but he is distraught at being out of the loop. Hirato meets family while he is in Rome. And Marco is not hosting the meeting, and somehow Marco feels like he let everyone down.

Marco makes cappuccinos, and plates some Italian pastries such as *Biscotti di Ceglie*, which have the taste of almond paste. He returns from the kitchen with two *Cassatella di sant'Agata*, a delicate pastry with a cherry on the top.

Hana finally appears relaxed. She explains that Kaito and Asuka are involved in the Akiya market. Rural decline in Japan is reaching outrageous levels, where something like one out of eight homes are being abandoned, and then re-sold for rock bottom prices. Kaito and Asuka purchase these homes, invest in their reconstruction, and then flip them for a decent profit. Kaito and Asuka have even begun to work as middlemen, finding Akiya locations, making short videos, and then advertising these homes globally. Americans and Europeans see the Akiya as positive, passive income-earners.

Mother and son have a meeting of minds; they gaze at the apartment together. Marco can see the emptiness of the space, and all the struggles they experienced living here.

There remain a lot of unanswered questions. Marco remains apprehensive about Aldo's motives. And because they have stopped talking, Marco has to find the truth. In fact, Marco recognizes that his uncle is taking some satisfaction knowing that his invitation for Serena to move will have a dramatic impact on Marco, too. Marco thrives at the challenge, knowing that his uncle's preoccupations are misplaced.

"What did youth think of that then?"

"I thought we need to be a little bit more respectable about your safety."

"You're not thinking outside the box. We have a human crisis and those were the faces of your brothers and sisters."

"I know."

"It breaks my heart. You know, I question God's motives just as much as anyone else. Just because you're His Holiness, doesn't mean you don't feel like blaming someone."

"I don't think this is a blame game."

"You're right. It is not a blame game, and truthfully, this is merely a process now: for we, as a people, to unite with science finally. For too long there has always been this tendency to separate the two, that one cannot help the other. But this is the time more than ever to show that science will hear our prayers. And science will provide us a miracle."

"Should I put that on Twitter today?"

"No, that sounds too audacious. We still need to stress the importance of prayer."

The sense of disengagement is overwhelming, as though anyone else in Marco's spot would speak the conversation over and over, burning the midnight oil all night long.

His Holiness goes over to a table and pours himself a cup of tea. He sits down and looks out the window. His Holiness remains a kind and generous man (Marco believes His Holiness is a great man). He sits with a contemplative disposition. And his greatness is reflective of all the things the two men have experienced together. Cardinal Peter's presence remains inside the room. Or the anecdotes he shares with the hospital staff. Or the exchanges with his security unit. They are reflected in his facial expressions, in his posture.

The domestic side of life will have ways to mitigate problems. Please do not try and compare our methods with how the domestics deal with their daily lives. It will not earn you any respect.

Cardinal Stewart zigzags through the windy streets in his new Peugeot. He listens to Chopin and assumes a friendly taxi driver demeanor. He spots a section on the street, with three or four restaurants to choose from, and randomly inquires which Chinese restaurant looks the best. It turns out the one they choose is one of the local's favorites.

The bell above the door announces a new customer, and Aldo even smiles at the fleeting attention. A young woman joins him, who wears jeans and a black tee, with the Eiffel Tower on the front. Aldo taps his cane after he notices Cardinal Stewart and Marco sitting in a booth at the back and decides to go over and say "hello".

"Funny seeing you here?"

"May I present Cardinal Stewart."

"I recommend the Egg Foo Yung."

Cardinal Stewart has ordered Kung Pao Chicken, and Peking Roast Duck. He raises his eyebrow at Marco inquiring if they need to order more.

"I'm just learning how to walk again. The spring rolls also, so I make the effort to come around whenever I can."

"I see."

"Did you have an accident?"

"You could say that. I rolled our car."

"I'll pray for you."

"Thank you, father."

Cardinal Stewart takes both of their hands and lowers his head, and the three men pray. After the cardinal finishes, Marco looks up and holds an evil look on his face. And he cannot let it go. The young woman comes over and taps Aldo on the shoulder, but he brushes her off as he tightens his grip on his cane. The cardinal knows something is amiss. He gently reaches across the table and taps Marco's hand.

"Your nephew is a glowing light who will help you through your struggles. Indeed, I can already see you are on the road to recovery."

"Perhaps in the physical sense, but I'm not sure I have been cured spiritually?"

All of the focus falls on Marco's shoulders. And these answers have been scripted for centuries. Indeed, inasmuch as the church has helped Marco, it will kindly show him the door. He looks across the table and gives a gentle dismissal, a push-away of sorts, of Cardinal Stewart's way of inviting Aldo towards a better life. But Marco does not have any inkling of how to help.

And Marco's sense of embarrassment has nothing to do with Aldo, but is rather due to Cardinal Stewart's ability to see the external confusion and embarrassment between Aldo and Marco. The cardinal's appraisal is spot on, and Marco suddenly tries to put his life in perspective.

Invariably, he is asked what kind of job he currently holds. And "in-between jobs" does not sound reassuring. And then, one day, his luck changes.

"I support anyone who is trying to improve the environment. Even though you work in the background, I can tell you stand for something. I see the same things that your new boss sees."

"Thanks. I appreciate that."

They have not grown close. The departure is rather boring. His Holiness is away on a trip. Marco leaves a card behind, but because of the security protocol, it is unlikely the card will come into His Holiness's possession.

"Could you at least thank His Holiness for everything he has done for me?"

"Of course, and I'm sure he would say the same to you. God bless you, son."

The Church has faced many storms before, and those who work within its walls are dedicated to outlasting the storm. And there are a lot of storms. They are experts at controversy. And they are experts at not caring.

From two hundred and sixty million Catholics in 1900 to over one billion today, the Catholic Church has expanded more in the last one hundred years than any time in its history.

Hana and Hirato enter the apartment.

On one side of the kitchen is a series of cabinets, white frames and frosted glass with gold handles. And on the other side is a series of shelves, without any covers, which look out of place in a kitchen.

A picture of His Holiness hangs on the wall. He washes the vegetables and places them in a glass bowl on the counter. Hana and Hirato suddenly appear, which compounds a sense of accomplishment over and over.

The different stages of life – say, moving into an apartment, meeting friends for drinks, going to a wedding – play on your senses. And then you get the call, and then you can go back to work again.

"This is a welcome home present."

Hana places the glasses on the table and Marco pours everyone a tall drink.

Hana puts sheets on the small couch and helps Hirato to lie down. She covers him in a blanket, and he falls asleep.

The young couple lie in the middle of the kitchen floor on a blow-up mattress. Marco lights a candle. Hana plugs in her iPhone and plays Leonard Cohen.

"It was a long day."

"I think this is the longest day we've ever had."

"I cannot believe we drank an entire bottle."

"Yeah. I think you need to watch how much you drink. You might end up like my father someday."

"Hana! I had four shots."

"You're slurring."

Marco could hear music in the distance.

"Turn off your phone."

A couple have an argument on the street, which escalates into shouts of laughter at the other person. This actually has a soothing, loving texture, and somehow, they have sparked some joy into the night.

Marco can hear music from outside. He waves at the candle, and it begins to flutter. The sounds of a distant opera swoon inside the room. Hana falls asleep. Marco turns onto his side and continues to listen to the music. Or else, there is a group outside deciding what they are going to do next. They are not sounds that belong to anyone except the rules that exist between the commitment to work and pay the rent. The sounds of the living. And he expects the same is true for all his neighbors. Marco feels the pressure of this place. He needs to protect the small apartment, the poorly insulated walls, and the awkward distance from the subway station.

Hana awakens from the light snoring. She goes into the living room and makes sure her dad is OK.

The radiance of a family who understands their role is tantamount to our success. And that is why we continue to operate worldwide.

The next morning, Serena arrives to find everyone still asleep. She places a plastic bag of fresh cherries on the counter. She lights a cigarette. She steps over the young lovebirds and puts fresh flowers in a vase and places them on the kitchen table. She sits at the kitchen table, drinks a Starbucks cappuccino, and smokes a cigarette. Moments later, Marco awakens and notices his mom filing her fingernails over a Kleenex on the kitchen table.

Giorgio was never really given much of a chance. He was spoiled rotten as a little boy. By the time he was ten, he was given two birthdays, just because he talked about it so much.

Nothing made sense to the young boy growing up. He could not understand why he was not allowed to play professional soccer. His mother explained that he could play soccer, but if he were to show up on a professional pitch, no one would recognize him. But Giorgio was relentless, and he came up with outlandish stories. He would follow the team, go to the airport, hide in garbage cans, whatever it took, and then, at kickoff, show up on the pitch so no one could say anything.

He started to get into fights at an early age. According to his teachers, he was never a bully, and never picked on anyone smaller than him. He was mostly defending himself from the older boys.

By the time Giorgio was sixteen, he had dropped out of school. He had accumulated a lot of street cred from all the fights he had won. By the time he was seventeen, he was focussed on being a gangster. He started to hang out at bars with his friends and spent all of his time getting into fights.

Some of his friends were already part of crews.

Meanwhile, he was crawling through the rafters above warehouses in the middle of the night, just to steal some microwaves.

One day, Giorgio robbed a deli, which was the biggest mistake of his life, since the owner caught a glimpse of him. He wore a beard for the next three years. One day, he shaved his beard, and entered the deli, where the owner said: "you're the bastard that robbed us."

He would sell fentanyl, and then discovered that he had ended up killing four of his cousins. He immediately stopped dealing drugs. He saw a psychiatrist and admitted that he used to sell drugs. The shrink said he intended to report Giorgio to the police, at which point Giorgio famously threatened to kill the psychiatrist. This became a big court case in the area, and eventually the judge dismissed the charges against Giorgio, but he never regained his reputation after that.

He found a job at a call centre as a customer service agent for a doughnut company. He mostly fielded calls about fundraising opportunities, or store hours, and sometimes customers would discuss their allergy concerns. There were also lots of strange calls from teenagers, asking him to list the ingredients in some of the popular doughnuts. Some callers would say things like they had found a finger in one of their doughnuts. One person claimed they were locked in the bathroom, and Giorgio had to call the retail outlet and speak to the manager. Sure enough, they found someone locked in the bathroom.

Giorgio figured out quite early that the free doughnut coupon was the key to success. And then, one day, he started to push back: "I like your story, but you are going to need to hire a field of lawyers before I can help you with that one."

Or else: "when you said you got into an argument with the cashier, did you really reach over the counter, grab her by the collar, and threaten to stick your fist down her throat?" Usually, the customer would just simply hang up, or else occasionally they would ask to speak to Giorgio's supervisor, the response to which was always: "all of the supervisors are dead today."

His manager, Amerigo, was asked to review some of Giorgio's calls. Instead of requesting to meet, he called the police. The police went over to his cubicle and politely escorted him out of the building.

"After listening to your calls, we have decided that you have a good chance of becoming a stand-up comedian. But if you remain here, the President might kill you."

"I understand."

Giorgio was unemployed and had a wife and two kids to feed. A friend obtained a phone directory for all the care homes for the elderly in Italy. The directory appeared to be quite useful, because, at the time, there were all sorts of scams targeting older people, which involved calling an elderly person, giving them a line about who was calling, and requesting payment for a non-existent service.

He hired a small group of trusted callers, and they went to work. They ended up bringing in over one hundred thousand euros in the first month alone.

The news of the operation made Giorgio a bit of a household name.

There were an equal number of mafia and police who were impacted by Giorgio's scam. In other words, it didn't help his situation with the mob. Quite the opposite

– he earned a reputation as someone who lacked respect and would take money from any angle he could find.

It was around this time that he met Serena. Her father was a well-known gangster in the area, as was her brother. Giorgio was pleased that he was able to finally meet someone like Serena, who he believed was going to give him the chance to succeed in the under-world, like he always dreamed. Serena never once mentioned her father, despite Giorgio constantly bringing up his name in conversations.

She made him feel as though he should be just as proud to date someone like herself, who was connected to all of these gangsters.

Giorgio started to have ideas of grandeur. He started to plot all sorts of crazy ideas, and then insisted that she should bring his ideas to the attention of Aldo. But Serena would have none of it. She told Giorgio that she was done with the business. But the plan backfired. Aldo was waiting. Aldo tackled him and threatened to put a bullet in the side of his head.

"But I want to make us both rich."

"I'm already rich. And you have a history of getting rich and then getting arrested. What is the point in supporting someone who will get us pinched?"

"That doesn't make sense, how am I to support myself?"

Aldo, who was incorrigible right down to the bone, ignored Giorgio's suggestions, and threatened to kill every member of his family if he came around anymore. Several weeks later, Giorgio's body was found in a river.

Hana checks her phone and notices a message from Boulder. She reads the message over and over. She brushes the screen with the edge of her thumb.

Marco sits at the kitchen table with his mother.

"How did you get in here?"

"I dated the landlord... back in the day."

"What?"

"Yeah, when you used to play soccer. I remember because I took him on a date to watch you play."

"What? What are you talking about?"

"I was knocking at your door, when he suddenly appeared. We talked. And then he let me in. I don't think he wanted his wife to know he was talking to me."

"OK?"

Roma Internet

Marco looks towards the street corner and notices a café. He sits down on the outside terrace. He has just picked up the local newspaper, when the waiter appears.

He is careful not to lay his eyes on the names of any of his favorite teams. He whips the pages until he reaches the entertainment section. He stops at the advert for *Greyhound* starring Tom Hanks. He checks which languages are available.

"A breakfast this morning, sir?"

"No, thank you, just a coffee and a *Sfogliatelle*."

"Very good."

He notices a young woman who sits a few tables away. She is bent over slightly as she checks her purse. She looks up and makes eye contact with Marco. Marco surmises it is an accident. She even appears to go back into her purse and check for something again.

But Marco continues to smile at her anyway. And when she turns back, Marco lifts his finger to his cheek and traces a big smile on his face. She gives him a snarky smile. But she is in no mood to flirt, and quickly grabs her cigarettes from the table and makes off up the street.

He climbs the steep, cement stairs and notices the gardeners standing in front. He smiles whenever one of the gardeners looks at him. He cannot afford a single false move.

He hears gunfire. He looks at the gardeners: nothing happens. There was no loud gunshot blast. Marco inflates his chest and continues towards the front doors. The building seems to soar forever into the sky. And then, he places his hand above his head and follows the side of the building back to ground level.

The building is silver metal with black windows. The Colosseum and Pantheon feel like they are in different cities. The windows provide a perfect reflection of the buildings along the street. It is as if all the buildings in the area converge in the same place. The reflections provide imaginative powers he did not know existed.

They are workmates. They've swapped shifts innumerable times, and brag to each other about their family lives. Life is the sports section of the magazine rack inside a cigar shop. Life is grander here.

It is time to go inside. He enters the front doors as if he has entered a very dark place. The shadows make things colder. The people around him appear to be more alive.

A large, rectangular display panel stands in front of the security desk, allowing customers to approach the panel and use the touch screen to find their destinations. The spacious lobby area, with glass walls, is bordered by a black leather couch.

Marco turns towards the elevators, and he notices the Roma Internet sign hanging from the ceiling. The wire stretches ten meters towards a buffed metal ceiling.

Marco speaks about his experience inside the Vatican, and the challenges he faced trying to build His Holiness's Twitter and Instagram numbers. They act very interested, and they are keen for Marco to apply the same strategies and try to boost the popularity of Roma Internet. Roma Internet feel very confident about their role in the marketplace; however, they must persuade different sectors to be more accepting of their offer. For example, the local government has strict laws pertaining to the use of towers, as does the Italian government. The board of directors is interested in learning how Marco can change the opinion of government. They accept that the challenges are difficult; however, lots of other countries have already succeeded at shifting government attitudes.

The bellhop at the hotel where Marco and Hana attended a technology conference takes a drag of his joint. And just when he is about to approach Marco and Hana, he decides to hold back. He contemplates leaving his job, which is why he smokes his joint so frantically. And the idea of not lugging luggage up to a room tomorrow gives him some extra umph. He cares little about his customers, the tips don't add up anymore.

And Hana has no wish to be friendly, for they are all being watched. And the Porky Pig mask scratches her face. And the Goofy mask is covered in sweat. Instead, they give thumbs-ups. And everyone is happy.

"I saw you at the conference."

"I remember you. Did you have a good time?"

"Yes, but I forgot to give you a fat tip!"

Everyone likes to go on vacation, particularly in another country. Marco thinks why not advertise Roma Internet in another country, and make it evoke the same emotions as a vacation pamphlet?

"For example, we can show the Eiffel Tower, and the French in all parts enjoying the broadband they have. And then switch to an Italian in France, looking at the Eiffel Tower. And then suddenly back in Roma, using his smart phone, looking at the photos they captured while they were in France."

"I like it. And it also shows that we love our neighbors."

"Exactly. It is all about diplomacy and becoming friends."

"This is going to work."

They discuss her recent divorce. Her only son, Carmichael, who is aged five, likes to go to the park and play with his friends. Recently, she bought a car.

"Perhaps I can take you for a drive sometime?"

Marco stands in the elevator and holds two coffees. He listens to the sounds of each passing floor. He watches the numbers descend. His phone begins to vibrate. He falls to his knees and places the coffees on the floor.

"I'm on my way right now."

"OK, I love you."

"Of course. I love you."

The door opens and he walks gingerly into the middle of the lobby. Hana takes one of the coffees. They head over to the black leather bench on the east side of the building and sit down.

"They will be here in two days. They are at the airport now."

"How could they be?"

"I told them I would call right back."

"Terrific."

The tables feel like a labyrinth, and his style of meeting, his gestures, his general approach are all courteous.

The arrivals area is full as two flights have arrived at the same time. Hana has finally come home. And Hirato takes her bag and leads them to the carousel. And finally, Hana can rest. She feels as though she has finally graduated.

There is some attempt to capture Marco's attention.

Kaito is about four foot eleven inches tall. And Asuka is about four foot five inches tall. The sharp suit and haute couture suggest they are fashion-conscious beyond the magazines. These are connoisseurs of high quality, who depend on mills to deliver the goods, or else. For better or worse, their tininess is so disturbing that it comes off as unique.

Kaito has a perfectly trimmed moustache. Asuka nods her outfit is Chanel. Of course. She does not gush about the diamonds.

They appear a little intimidated, but Marco changes his disposition and makes everyone feel at ease.

"Do you want a Scotch to start?"

"Yes, a nice Scotch would be perfect."

Kaito and Asuka are an inseparable couple. Whenever there was a family function, they would appear and offer Hirato a gift of money. Or else, Hana would hear stories about Kaito and Asuka from her mom or dad. They were always sordid stories. Hirato would go on about Kaito's bad temper. He had a tendency to get into fights whenever he went out. Hana never understood what that meant. Hirato hosted an end-of-tour event at a karaoke bar, and Kaito and Asuka appeared. Kaito got in a serious fight with another table. What had triggered the fight was unknown, but it spilled over into the streets, and suddenly knives were being used. The two men fought until they could hear sirens.

A young gun had been trying to make his name in the business, whatever that meant. And he tested his luck on

Kaito. This newbie, who they referred to as "the Kid", is now making lots more money and has even begun working as security for local celebrities. One night, Kaito decided he wanted to go out for drinks. He noticed the Kid walking into a corner store. The biggest challenge in the altercation was getting the security tape, and then finding a back exit to avoid the CCTV. It took him forever to find Asuka. They ended up going for drinks and watching the police investigation from the window of the bar. Everyone knew it was Kaito behind the murder, but not one person said anything.

Next, Kaito turned to the entertainment sector. Soon after, he was walking around movie sets in Tokyo. And then in Australia. And, before long, he was taking meetings in Cannes. However, by the time he reached Cannes, he was no longer some hood twisting arms to get a producer credit. Kaito was staying up late, going over scripts and locking locations. And breaking into his actors' and actresses' homes, ensuring they were eating right, or sleeping with the right people. He made Harvey Weinstein look like a couch potato. And then, he did something which Harvey forgot to do – when word got out that the producer was out of control, he took a third-rate actor and hanged him from a bridge outside of Tokyo. They plastered his handiwork on the front page of the local newspaper. Even the *Hollywood Reporter* ran the story. Kaito was interviewed, during which he said: "I never met the man, but I was going to put him in my next picture. What a shame he died!"

He got rich fast. He was not accountable for the violent decisions of his past. And his present and future would be a bed of roses, because his business operated on fear. The movie business became very lucrative, but then he started to drift away.

Real estate was a natural fit. And real estate was a little more glamorous than Hollywood. The movies were specialized power. But everyone who is rich is interested in real estate. Whereas not everyone wants to get into the movies. He set up a real estate company and began to sell properties all over Japan. And then, he began pursuing buyers from other countries, who were interested in investing in Japan. He enjoyed a shock wave of growth shortly after. Because an investor from another country was such a big risk, they must have had more assets tucked away somewhere. Naturally, that was when he went into overdrive, and frauded hundreds of customers out of hundreds of millions of yen, keeping them tied up in real estate deals.

They travel the world, wear the best clothes, and dangle the best jewellery. They host parties. They are invited to royal weddings. They are given VIP seats at inaugurations. They are part of the rich and famous. They have assumed the happy face of organized crime.

Despite their economic successes, Kaito and Asuka remain a mystery. The Yakuza could not claim them as one of their own, even though Kaito was constantly doing deals with them. He does deals in Europe and North America with unknown persons and groups, which earns them a healthy profit. Their reputation grows, but there is an aura of doubt and mystery about their success. In other words, not everyone likes the fact that they are rising through the ranks of prestige, because they are not helping out some of the other major players.

Kaito knows that Hirato was a one-time member of the Yakuza gang, who decides to distance himself from the criminal world. However, he knows that one does not simply leave a life of crime: it stays with one one's whole life. Also, Kaito knows that Hirato is a huge source of valuable information. Hirato knows all the major contacts in Japan and Europe and has spent lots of time in North America. Most importantly, Hirato is still respected. Hirato was such an enforcer and earned the Yakuza so much money that his time with the group is considered a valuable "growth period". Indeed, the Yakuza still earns money from the different business ventures that Hirato started.

And what's more, Hirato is at a place where he is still enamored by his former self. What better way to get back into the business than by consulting his nephew, and then taking a cut of the business choices that his nephew makes along the way? It is a win-win situation.

Suddenly, the story begins to get complicated, because Hirato cannot figure out his daughter's relationship with Marco. He cannot figure out whether they are trying to cover up what happened in Boulder, or whether they are in it for the long-term.

Hana orders drinks. Marco goes into detail about his travel campaign that they plan to shoot in the Swiss Alps.

"You immediately feel jealous and want to be there."

"Yes, and those are the signals we are trying to send to the Italian government. We want them to know that Italians want broadband internet in every region of our country."

"That's great."

Hana nods approvingly.

The four-star reputation requires one to live in Japan for numerous generations to truly appreciate the sumptuousness. Marco is tired and does not want to go out dancing. Marco insists that Hana should join her cousins, but she wants to return home. They plan to meet tomorrow night.

Marco and Hana return home. But Marco insists that Hana should go out to the club and meet her cousins. Finally, Hana admits that Kaito and Asuka are meeting some friends, which works to end the conversation.

Marco undresses and doesn't speak. But there is something in the air, and Marco is not entirely sure what it all means.

He goes to the kitchen and returns a few moments later. Hana is on her phone, but she quickly ends the call when Marco appears. But there is now some tension and suddenly Marco must decide.

They make love.

Hana changes into her nightgown. They get into bed.

Kaito and Asuka are in Rome to explore business opportunities. They have amassed a small fortune in Tokyo. And they are interested in investing in other countries now.

The story sounds legitimate, but Marco can't understand why they need to suddenly make money in another country. Marco explains all the legal differences with owning in Italy, and the huge autocratic barriers that stand in the way. Not to mention the business etiquette, which, of course, would disappear eventually, but appears as a challenge at the outset. Or else living in Rome as a foreigner, and the difficulties with learning a new language.

Indeed, Marco is exhausted by the discussion. All the things they have discussed are either unimportant or else will be dealt with on the fly. In other words, they have already decided they want to do business in Italy.

"But, why Rome?"

"Because that is where you live."

The words float in the air. And suddenly, Marco appears confused by the comment. He does not get the connection between himself and Hana's cousins' business dealings. Except that they are finally family, and it is natural that they would want to be close to their family.

"I think it would be wise to have successful venture capitalists as friends."

"Yes, and they want to be powerful and important."

Marco is puzzled by the comment. But they are too tired to discuss the matter anymore.

"My father will guide them."

And suddenly, Marco does not know what to say.

"We should have gone out dancing."

Juanita, the secretary, enters the office and explains that the Swiss shoot has changed once more. Marco must decide if he wants to go for a medium, recognizable name or instead have a fifteen-second advert.

Marco stares at her legs while he speaks.

"A great script without a star is a good movie. But a bad script with a great star is a great movie."

"Does that mean we go with the medium recognized star?"

"Did they give us any names yet?"

"No."

"I don't watch Italian cinema, but yes, we'll go for the star. You know what, Juanita: I learnt that in Boulder."

"Who?"

"Boulder Colorado. I think I'm right about this one.

Might be the first time."

Juanita wears a Missoni, sleeveless mini dress and a gold chain. Her manner of laughing shimmers like an expensive accessory.

Marco goes around his desk, and sits comfortably in his thick, leather chair, and holds the arms like they are lifting up towards the clouds.

When the phone begins to ring, he looks up at Juanita once more, who has turned to the side. She places her hand on her wrist and looks out into the hallway.

"I got all this knowledge from Boulder, Colorado."

"Yeah?"

"I'm going to take you there someday."

"OK."

Roma Internet receives news that the Italian government wants to meet to discuss the new strategy. It dawns on Marco that he requires one expensive suit.

Marco stands in the middle of the sidewalk and looks up at the Italian Suits sign. Marco whispers "Dolce & Gabbana, Gucci, and Giorgio Armani" under his breath.

The sky has a dark, gloomy look about it. As Marco looks upward, he searches for something interesting to see, as a way to continue the conversation with Hirato. Even though they have trouble communicating, at least they can share something sacred from the skies.

The storm-like sky includes a white cloud that appears out of place. The sky is begging to rain, to storm, to unleash some discomfort on everyone. These random white clouds, decoys, will soon be shattered.

But Marco is not moved by these weather anomalies. He looks forward to putting something on his Visa, improving his look, increasing the status of the group.

But the sky is far too dangerous to accept a simple shrug. Because the sky can push crowds under an awning, force little yelps from unsuspecting targets, who smack the walls of office buildings with heavy, drenched newspapers. This is where someone in a cashmere sweater decides to stand in the middle of the street and look up and randomly sing songs from the Broadway Songs Essential compilation. Somehow, a sidetracked playwright catches on, but scampers away, for his hubris is already crafted with another pretty girl in mind.

The showroom has a marble floor and fresco ceiling. A rack of blazers is placed strategically in the middle of the room. The walls are designed with custom-made shelves, which hold shirts and ties and accessories. Marco holds Hana's hand. Hirato finds a comfortable chair near the front entrance beside a table with walking canes. Marco enters the back room. There is a glass door to the outside, which appears to be unused. There is an air conditioner above the door that blows cold air into the room. There is a feeling of freshness and intrigue inside the room.

He must choose between a brown suit and several navy-blue suits. They are each forty long and single breasted. The salesman insists on the first brown suit; however, Marco cannot decide because he doesn't think he has enough shoes that will match a brown suit. Moreover, Marco thinks he will get more wear out of a navy suit.

Finally, the salesman, who is stout with a wide girth, grabs a copy of *Vogue Hommes* from the showroom and rips out one of the pages with men in blue suits.

This is the kind of suit that already assumes a lengthy

history of memories, even if they are not the owner's per se. In other words, the brown, which is subdued teetering towards green, reflects a history of elegance. It might have been a supper jacket at a fancy Upper East Side restaurant, or else the jacket of a gallery owner who made an appearance at the famous photographer's vernissage. The jacket signals strength and survival, and you are part of the group of men who think this item is more essential than the little black dress. Indeed, you are upholding trends as you go along. And recall this item has been worn numerous times, in numerous places, with less ambitious goals than your own.

The waistcoat is double-breasted, which gives it another level of elegance, and it has black leather buttons. And the shoulder construction is classic: not too puffy to make you stand out. Indeed, the browns are coming back with a vengeance. The suit of choice of your grandparents' generation is easy for any complexion, and it tends to pop a little extra with a snazzy tie. A chest pocket square will put you over the top.

"My dog has a blue suit. My sister's child: she is eight months pregnant, and he has a blue suit! Real men wear brown suits. Or tan suits. Or grey suits."

Hana agrees with the salesman; however, Marco is not convinced. Nor does he think that ripping out the pages of the *Vogue Hommes* is a very smart idea.

"I think you ruined a perfectly good magazine. Over nothing."

"Over nothing! I go through ten of these every day. It is the best piece of sales investment I've ever made!"

"OK, I'll take the brown suit."

Marco takes the suit and puts it over his arm. He finds Hana, who is looking at the suspenders, and takes her hand. They walk towards the exit. Hirato sits on the edge of his chair and holds a polite grin. No one is in any race to go outside. He looks over Hana's shoulder at the salesman at the cash register. Then at the ceiling fan, which is turning, but has a very noticeable click every couple of seconds.

"Can you ask your father a question for me?"

"Of course."

"Ask him if he will let me buy him a suit, for all the wonderful things you've done for me?"

Hana speaks to her father. Next, she turns adoringly to Marco and gently nods "yes".

Marco returns to the showroom at the back of the store. Hirato starts to follow, and as he peers up towards the showroom, he sees Marco raise his arms into the air...

Postscript

Hana sits at her bedside and listens to the sounds outside, like Marco once did. Serena walks across the hallway, and closes the bedroom door. Hana can hear Serena in the background talking to Aldo.

Hana recalls the anger that Marco would display whenever Aldo came over to drop off some money for Serena. She holds the rosary tightly. She wonders if that is her job now that Marco is dead. Should she start to act defiant towards Aldo? Or should she tell Serena that she thinks it is unfair the way in which Aldo treats her?

After Marco died, Aldo turned very angry towards Hana and Hirato. Indeed, there were times when Hana thought her life was in danger.

But the trial changed all of that.

The district attorney brought conspiracy to commit murder charges against Hirato. Hana was interviewed, but they decided not to prosecute because they did not have enough evidence. The mere fact that Hana was interviewed was enough for Aldo to assume she was guilty.

Aldo attended the trial every day. The courtroom had light wooden wainscoting and the walls were a flat olive green. There were long benches covered in red leather. During the course of the two-month trial, while Aldo listened to the evidence against Hirato, his anger grew so strong that once a court officer came over to him and asked if he was going to be OK.

Hirato's trial revealed that he was a major player in the Yakuza, and that he ran numerous illegal companies back in Japan. The problem, however, was that running illegal companies is not the same as conspiracy to commit murder. Accordingly, the charges against Hirato were dropped. He quickly rushed back to Japan.

Hana decided to remain in Rome because she no longer respected her family. Hirato has not disowned his daughter, but he feels very upset that she did not support him during the trial.

Once Hana discovers that Kaito and Asuka are the ones behind Marco's murder, she blames herself for not protecting Marco during this troubling time. Hana recalls Marco asking her why Kaito and Asuka were in Rome? And why they were pursuing business opportunities in a country where they didn't speak the language? Hana was in the habit of deflecting questions because she genuinely thought they were pursuing legitimate business opportunities. Marco could see right through her lies.

Consequently, Marco considered leaving Hana. He explored his feelings towards Juanita at the office. However, after he sat with Hana on the long leather couch inside Roma Internet, he realized she had no idea what was going on around them. And their love was real.

Hana enters the living room and sits down on the couch. She turns on the TV. Of course, Serena continues to have a busy social life, and despite losing Marco, she carries on with her friends from the neighborhood. Indeed, her friends have made the transition of losing a son appear acceptable. Even though that might sound strange to most people, Serena and the others knew too well the tight rope that Marco was walking.

Indeed, the moment he chose to leave his job at the Vatican, Serena knew his days were numbered. His departure from the Church was the moment she prayed for a miracle. She stretched her prayer as far and as wide as you can imagine. But she only found misery. She accepts her emptiness and takes comfort in being around compassionate people.

Serena worked her entire life steering Marco towards a better life, different from the business choices of Aldo. But Marco was incorrigible. He loved his mother, but he rarely took her advice.

Serena stands behind the couch and smiles at Hana before speaking.
"What are you doing tonight?"
"Watching a movie on my iPad."
"Don't you think you've watched enough movies?"
"No."

The trial in Italy exposed a lot of Hirato's business dealings, which has prompted considerable attention from authorities in Japan. Accordingly, most days Hirato works tirelessly with lawyers to protect his business operations. His network of connections seeks out legitimate companies to help Hirato hide his companies' assets.

Hirato barely goes out, save to work in the backyard, where he continues to share his famous miso recipe with his neighbors. One neighbor is in talks about opening a restaurant in Hirato's name.

Hirato hired Kaito and Asuka to come to Rome and kill Marco. After Marco left the showroom, the salesman went over to the door that led to the alleyway and unlocked the door. Marco returned to the showroom, where Kaito shot Marco twice in the chest.

In the end, Hirato was always concerned about power. And how to save the power he had amassed in his lifetime. He knew that Hana was going to be a big shot. After all, she was his only daughter now, and he had taught her everything he knew. And it was only a matter of time before he would introduce Hana to the realities of the family business. But the Boulder job changed everything. Hirato did not count on Hana falling in love with someone like Marco. What's more, Marco was pursuing a lucrative career. He was going to be much bigger than Hirato could ever imagine.

Killing Marco was easy because his power was so great. Stopping him was available to anyone who wanted to protect their own power. The fact that Marco was making strides in dealing with the government also began to attract attention. Not to mention he still had contacts at the Vatican. Hirato was very keen to protect his own power, especially considering the family dynamics of an only daughter. The prospect of losing her to someone in another country was the final straw.

In the middle of the night, Aldo barges into the apartment. Serena screams and tries to restrain him. Aldo breaks through her arms, and smashes through Hana's door.

"Who is Martin?"

"I don't know what you are talking about?"

As Hana sits up, the rosary falls to the floor. Serena waves her arms wildly and paces in the background.

"He asked to speak to me about Marco."

Hana turns on the bedside lamp. She tries to get her hair out of her face.

"They were friends. That's all. They met a few times."

Hana starts to cry. Aldo grabs her shoulders and starts to shake her like a madman.

"Martin knows nothing about Marco. He doesn't know about the family?"

Serena appears in the doorway. She holds a gun. She fires a shot. The room turns black.

"Let her go."

In the darkness, Aldo gets off the bed and goes towards the front doorway. He turns and looks at his sister. He is unable to speak.

"Get out of our apartment."

Kaito has seen an uptick in his business dealings. Hirato is aggravated by their relationship, as Kaito did not have to experience a lengthy trial. Moreover, Hirato has become paranoid believing that he is being watched by authorities. In other words, Kaito and Asuka hold considerable power over Hirato in terms of their connection with Marco's murder. If word gets out that they were the hired contract killers, Hirato could be sent to jail in a snap.

One day, Hirato sits in his backyard with Kaito and Asuka, when Midori comes outside and says someone by the name of Martin is here to see Hirato.

Hirato does not know who Martin is. Nor does anyone

else at the meeting. Martin tells Midori that he is a friend of Hana's, and that she had asked him to send a message on her behalf.

Hirato, who misses his daughter greatly, finds the request a touch strange, but given Martin is a Westerner, and he appears to know a great deal about Hana, he welcomes him into his home.

Martin removes his shoes and walks gently down the hallway, past the tatami room, through the kitchen, and into the backyard.

Martin wears jeans and a Mexican poncho and baseball cap, with a skull and roses patch, the logo of the Grateful Dead.

The two men speak for several minutes, and it appears they are getting along OK.

Martin explains his relationship with Marco: "He was not only a friend, but the person that allowed me to get up in the morning."

"I don't understand what you mean?"

"I mean, I am here to revenge his death."

"I was with him at the store. I did not kill him."

Hirato looks behind Marco and sees Midori speaking to Kaito in the kitchen.

"Let's say you are right. What would be solved if you killed me?"

Kaito leaves the house.

Martin puts a bullet into the side of Hirato's head. He dies instantly.

Midori rushes outside and kneels down beside Hirato and cries into his hands which lie on his chest.

"You could have stopped Hirato from killing Marco."

"I know."

"His mother hosted your husband and made him meals."

"They were going to kill Hana. The Boulder crew did this."

The Book is designed to lift you up when your domestic resources have left you out in the cold.

"Marco could have helped you."

Martin steps onto the residential street. The street is on the side of a hill, which allows for views of the surrounding area. Martin can see the Metro running along a disappearing track. Suddenly, a young woman approaches him. She appears to be holding a selection of colorful flowers.

Asuka fires two shots.

As Martin lies on the damp sidewalk, Asuka can hear Kaito laughing and telling her to get in the car.

The couple sit in the car for a moment. Asuka wipes the fog from the passenger side window and gazes at Martin one last time. Kaito starts to pull away, heavy on the clutch, indicating a lack of concern.

The police have barricaded the street. A police helicopter scours the area for anything suspicious.

Midori sits in the tatami room. A police investigator sits opposite Midori. He reads his notes after interviewing some of the neighbors, who all have a different story. Another police officer closes the *shoji*, providing some privacy for the interrogation. The investigator looks at Midori, and suddenly he feels cold, not knowing where to begin.

The End

About The Author

Jeremy Rafuse is from Canada. He was born in Toronto, grew up in Winnipeg and later Saskatoon. He also lived in Montreal.

Jeremy was nominated for Best Screenplay at the Beverly Hills Film Festival three times and was once a Quarter-Finalist at the Zoetrope Screenplay Contest. He is the author of the crime novel *280* and most recently *The Red Zone Speeches*.

Jeremy currently lives in Paris, France, where he is completing his PhD in philosophy. He is also working on his third novel.

https://jeremyrafuse.wordpress.com/
https://www.instagram.com/jeremyrafuse.author/

www.blossomspringpublishing.com

www.ingramcontent.com/pod-product-compliance
Lightning Source LLC
Chambersburg PA
CBHW031324170626
46807CB00002B/565

BIN TRAVERLER FORM

Cut By: Wilfredo Hernandez   **Qty** 32   **Date** 7-6-26.

Scanned By: _____ **Qty** _____ **Date** _____

Scanned Batch ID's

_____ _____

Notes / Exceptions

_____